D0109483

FOR GRACE RECEIVED

Valeria Parrella

FOR GRACE RECEIVED

*Translated from the Italian
by Antony Shugaar*

Europa
editions

Europa Editions
116 East 16th Street
New York, N.Y. 10003
www.europaeditions.com
info@europaeditions.com

Translation by Antony Shugaar
Original title: *Per grazia ricevuta*
Translation copyright © 2009 by Europa Editions

Library of Congress Cataloging in Publication Data is available
ISBN 978-1-933372-94-5

Parrella, Valeria
For Grace Received

Winner of the Zerilli-Marimò/City of Rome Prize
for Italian Fiction 2006.
This translation was made possible thanks to kind support
from the Zerilli-Marimò/City of Rome Prize fund.

Book design by Emanuele Ragnisco
www.mekkanografici.com
Cover illustration © by Giovanni Binel

The drawing on page 63 is from: Crockett Johnson, Barnaby, Dover
Publications, Inc., New York © Crockett Johnson, 1942, 1943.

Prepress by Plan.ed – Rome

Printed in Canada

CONTENTS

RUN

To Tonino, for the bracelet.

E very time I cross this street, I always choose the same
spot: I walk sort of kitty-corner from the traffic
island, or straight as an arrow along the crosswalk, as
if the cars had stopped to let me pass. Or else, stepping
down from the trolley, without an umbrella, I run to take
shelter under the awning outside the pharmacy. But I always
cross Via Marina at this same spot, I don't do it on purpose—that is, I do it on purpose, but without wanting to.
And when I cross here, I imagine it. I imagine it so intensely
that I can see it: Mario, coming along the sidewalk. Not
crossing the street: it was already baking hot, so hot that a
body would automatically choose to walk in the shade. He
was walking fast, skimming along the windows of the Loreto hospital on his left, with the street advancing against the
waterfront on his right. The sea poised against the barracks
building, against the employment office, against the cranes
in the harbor. Mario was moving along briskly, as briskly as
the gentleman who had withdrawn money from the cash
machine a few seconds before, just as Mario was passing the
bank, walking quickly, then passing Sofas & Co. and
Château d'Ax. The gentleman from the cash machine was
just a few steps behind him, wearing the expression of a cash
withdrawal in a city you don't trust. Mario was expressionless, absolutely expressionless. He was walking fast, avoiding

the tree roots that were bulging up from beneath the sidewalk, walking to the right of the roots, on the street side. The ATM guy was walking to the left of the trees, on the hospital side, as if by staying as far from the street as possible he could ward off a mugging, as if the motorbike he feared might think twice before climbing the curb.

The shade has only a few trees to work with. They were erupting beneath the asphalt as Mario moved along past them: the last tree in the line was huge, and there was only a narrow space between its trunk and the wall. Mario passed through, touching the bark as he passed, and then there were no more trees. Three steps in the baking heat, eyes fixed on the awning where he would plunge back into the shade. He stepped down from the curb at a safe spot: where the emergency room entrance used to be there was now a construction site, and cars could no longer get through, so there was no need to look both ways when crossing the street. Three steps for Mario took a little more than a second. The gentleman from the cash machine heard the roar of a motor passing too close, felt a gust of air, and noticed an outstretched arm as he turned. He froze in terror, clutching at his trouser pocket, as the motorbike zipped past him and the passenger, the only one wearing a helmet, stabbed Mario between the shoulder blades with a six-inch blade. Then, as if he were clapping his arm around Mario's shoulder as they headed off together for an espresso in a nearby café, he searched Mario all over, pulled something out of his pocket, and climbed back onto the motorbike. The bike moved off, unhurriedly, toward Sant'Erasmo.

Knives are strange weapons. Luisa swears that it doesn't hurt, that when the blade slides into your flesh you barely notice; as she told me this, she ran her hand over her right thigh; along the length of her thigh ran twenty-seven stitches and a line of white scar tissue. And in fact, a knife is a weapon made to be used on legs, not shoulders. It's meant to hurt you, not kill you. If you die of a stab wound, it's usually by mistake, because the blade sliced through the wrong vein in a knife fight. At the soccer stadium, or on the Mergellina waterfront in the chaos of New Year's Eve, when a snort of coke costs ten euros and even the poorest of the poor can afford one. If someone was going to kill him from behind, Mario would have expected a handgun.

When I imagine it, my back muscles tighten till they're stiff, and then my neck hurts for half a day.

The emergency room entrance was under construction; they were doing repairs on the access ramps. They dispatched an ambulance from a side street, though they could easily have lifted Mario up and carried him inside. The gentleman from the ATM sat down on the ground, but not right next to Mario: one step away, exactly the same distance he had been walking behind him, a yard or so before it happened, on the curb by the sidewalk. He sat there, leaning against the tree, until he saw the medical technicians hoist him into the ambulance; then he stood up and walked through a side entrance into the emergency room where they had taken Mario.

He was the first person I saw when I got there: he was sitting on a bench, resting his head and back against the wall.

"I can't let you bring him in here. He's too small."

"Don't be ridiculous, Doc," I said to the male nurse,

slipping past him on one side. "Where am I supposed to leave him?"

"Only children twelve or older are allowed in here."

"Okay, I understand that part; what am I supposed to do: wait until he turns twelve?"

I gave him a last-chance smile. If he didn't take that chance, I was ready to overturn the gurney on the left, the one parked against the wall.

The gentleman from the ATM stood up from his bench.

"Are you with the victim?"

"Yes."

"I can take care of your boy, go on in, don't worry."

Tonino was already beaded with sweat.

"Don't let the boy get worked up, mister."

Then I looked at the male nurse.

"Don't let this gentleman out of your sight, you. Understood? I'm holding you personally responsible."

Not much happens in the intensive care unit; they let you in so you can see he's still breathing, that they weren't lying to you when they said he was still alive. But that body there wasn't Mario. Mario was already out of the picture.

As I left the ICU, I knew one thing: Mario was alive, but in critical condition. Tonino had stretched out on the bench and fallen asleep, his head resting on the man's leg.

"Are you the wife?"

Instinctively, I said yes, and as I said it, I slowly, carefully turned my ring so that the stone was tucked away, hidden in the palm of my hand.

"Signora, if you like, I'd be glad to drive you home. My car is parked outside the pharmacy."

"Thanks, but home is all the way out in Ponticelli."

The doctors had given the man from the ATM the first reports on Mario's condition; they had given him a bag with the contents of Mario's pockets; later, they had taken the bag back. The police had told him not to leave the hospital, asked for his ID, told him he would have to talk to a detective and to come by the headquarters in Via Cosenz sometime tomorrow. The man from the ATM sat down on the bench, forgetting even that he was a smoker, watching me appear at the end of the corridor the way a cashier waits for her replacement at the end of the shift. And then, with Tonino sleeping on his leg, he began to calm down, slowing his breathing to match the boy's, until it was normal.

Now, I was going to make sure he explained what had happened.

That was the only reason I was in his car; I don't need rides from strangers; no one's ever driven me anywhere. I had Tonino in my belly and swollen legs, and I still stood on the sidewalk, waiting for traffic to move and the trolley to arrive. Once I was aboard, I shook boys roughly by the shoulder: that seat is for me.

Anyway, that man wasn't going anywhere. He couldn't just drop me off at the front door of my apartment building and leave. He hadn't said a word to me in the car.

"Come on up."

"No, thanks."

"I'm not asking you if you want to come up. I want an explanation."

"From *me*? If there's explaining to be done, I'd expect it from you."

"Are you joking, mister? My husband is flat on his back

in the ICU . . . what more do I need to tell you? You were there: what happened?"

"Bear with me, Signora. I must still be in a state of shock . . ."

"What, did somebody stab you, too?"

"No . . ."

"Then come on, let's go upstairs."

I took off my shoes. Ever since I was fourteen, I've never bought a pair of shoes with less than two-and-a-half inch heels. It seems that with heels under two-and-a-half inches, I can't get people to take me seriously. And if you want people to open their crotches and armpits to your tweezers, trust is everything.

But I took off my heels that day. I wanted to understand.

"I'm making some pasta for the boy . . . you want something to eat?"

"I couldn't eat. My stomach's tied in a knot."

"Okay, do as you like. I have to feed the boy, if you're hungry, have some for yourself."

As I stood with my back to him, he told me what happened, then he asked: "What does your husband do?"

"Jesus, where do you live? He's a courier . . . what do you do?"

"I have an umbrella shop, in the Via Toledo."

"All right then, you're a businessman, you should know certain things."

"Sure, Signora, but it's one thing to know them, quite another to do them . . . a money runner?"

"What do you mean?"

"Is money what your husband delivers?"

"Madonna, he delivers what needs delivering. He doesn't deal drugs. He guards the shipments, he makes sure they get where they're supposed to."

"And does he carry money?"

"Why would he?"

"Then why were they searching his pockets, those people?"

"Drugs."

"And why did they stab him? Were they junkies?"

"Hey, I was hoping you could tell me that. I have no idea. But sooner or later, it'll come out."

The man from the ATM came to the Loreto hospital every afternoon at three, visiting hour. He'd wait for me on the fire escape, smoking with the male nurses, while I stood, doing nothing, outside the entrance of the ICU. At 4:15, they'd let me in for twenty minutes, and he'd wait for me, downstairs, in his car, while I was doing nothing in the ICU. And he'd drive me home. On the days I couldn't get my next-door neighbor to babysit Tonino, I'd bring him with me, and I knew he was in good hands. While I waited, the two of them would go to the bridge over the Circumvesuviana commuter train tracks and watch as trains left the station.

Once, after the hospital, he took us out for a pizza in the Piazza Carità.

"It's just a short walk, if you want to see my umbrella shop."

"No, really, it's late, tomorrow is Tonino's last day of school. You've already been too kind, Signore . . ."

"Anna, why the formality? We see each other every day."

"Mamma, I could skip school, I don't mind."

"Tonino, don't be ridiculous. And you, too, do me a favor, don't talk nonsense."

I went to the hospital to kill time. The doctors wouldn't talk to me, and it wasn't just because I wasn't his wife. They figured they'd already told me everything I was capable of understanding. What's more, they seemed to think that he was taking up medical care that should be going to other patients. For someone with a stab wound in the back, he was getting more than his share of oxygen.

I was starting to lose clients. If a beautician stops working in the summer months, she can kiss her business good-bye. All the same, I was there every day at three in the afternoon, and I wouldn't leave until I had seen him.

"Why do you always come so early? You know we won't let you in until 4:15 anyway."

"Oh, and now it's up to you to decide what I can and can't do with my afternoons, is it? No . . . explain to me how that works . . ."

And then one morning, normal air was enough for him, and Mario woke up. His eyes were blue.

No one had bothered to let me know, so when I showed up outside the ICU, the male nurse told me Mario had been transferred to a regular ward. But the minute I saw him, I knew he was gone. It just wasn't him anymore, with that blank stare. Because in all my life, I've never been as beautiful as when Mario looked at me. From that point on, I could finally do something real to help him: bring frittatas in thermos packs and little fruit-juice bottles filled with coffee; empty his bedpan once he had regained control of his body; and rub Johnson's baby oil on his hips, massaging him to ward off bed sores, because flat on his back he couldn't breathe anymore.

*

As soon as Mario regained consciousness, the man from the ATM vanished. And in the meanwhile, Capisante sent for me. The first thing he asked was how Mario was doing, how his recovery was going. He asked me whether that gentleman who spent so much time with me knew anything, whether I knew anything, and whether Mario had given me anything. I told him that the gentleman was interested in dating me, and that Mario had left me with nothing more than a hand to cover my front and another to cover my behind. Only then did he tell me that he knew who had stabbed him: they were renegades, a splinter group of the system trying to set up in business for themselves. They were hijacking small shipments, biding their time until they could step up to the big time. I asked him the only thing that kept bothering me:

"Why didn't he shoot?"

"Because he wasn't carrying a gun."

Capisante noticed the flame that couldn't quite light my cigarette; he reached out and placed a hand on mine to steady it.

"In peacetime, no one goes armed outside of the quarter. What if the police stopped him on a random check? Is it worth the risk?"

"What if they killed him?"

"Anna, the guys who robbed him knew he wasn't armed: if they hadn't, would they have gone near him with a knife?"

"And anyway, we've taken care of them," he told me. Then, as a farewell gesture, he had one of his guys drive me home; when we got there, the young man pulled a wicker chest out of the trunk and carried it upstairs. Inside was pasta, cheese, sugar, and coffee. And eight hundred thousand lire in a plain white envelope. Everything that I had told him, Capisante already knew. As for the idea that Mario had been revenged: probably Capisante had managed to suppress a mutiny, to maintain his dominance, and if there was revenge it was strictly a secondary consideration, just like Mario and me. Still, I was pleased that he had summoned me: being the mother of his son still counted for something then.

Even on the medical floor, it was as if Mario was in a coma: he never said much to me, he put up no objections to anything that was done to him, and no one knew—or no one had bothered to ask—whether he would ever leave that hospital on his own two legs. When the guy from the ATM showed up again one day to see me, we went to the Bar Loreto to drink an espresso.

"You want that hot?" asked the barista.

And that's when I realized it was October, I should have pulled out the winter clothes and put away the summer clothes, and I'd forgotten to enroll Tonino in school.

"If you give me a power of attorney, I can go. But, of course, if you give me a power of attorney, then you'll have to tell me that the child has your last name, and that you're not even married."

I didn't have to explain anything to him: he knew perfectly well that when I came back home to Ponticelli, with thirty years behind me and a man who hadn't yet made up his mind how long he had left to live, my only option was to put on a pair of the highest heels I owned, strengthen my ankles, and tell everyone I met that I was married.

"Roberto, who told you?"

"The prosecutor. I had to appear yesterday for the investigation; I came to tell you about it."

"They've been questioning me too. But not the prosecutor."

"Capisante?"

"Mmm."

"Was he looking for something?"

"Why, do you have something that they would be asking me about?"

"No, what do you mean? I'm asking you because I don't have any idea how this sort of thing works."

Actually, neither did I, at least not the details, but it was becoming increasingly clear to me that Roberto was hiding something from me. At the same time, I knew that the only course of action open to me, unless I had some kind of death wish, was to trust him. And I wanted to trust him: I needed a rest.

"There's something I'd like you to do, but I don't know if I dare to ask."

"Anna, if you won't even tell me what it is, how can I say?"

"Could you talk to the doctors? To me, they won't explain how things stand."

"Then why would they say anything to me?"

"Because you know how to ask."

That's how I found out that the only real question was: where? We needed to decide on the best place to let him die. Mario had no family, except for the wife he had left to be with me, two months after their wedding, and now it was anybody's guess where she was. I asked Capisante to take care of it, somebody signed some papers, and Mario came back to his own bed where it was only right—everyone agreed—that he should die.

Instead, Mario lived on in that bed for seven months; meanwhile, at school, Tonino had almost learned to read.

When Tonino was one year old, the social worker who had arranged for me to be assigned the apartment set a cup and a little ball in front of him.

"Put the ball in the cup," she said to him with a smile.

Tonino looked at her, then he grabbed the cup by the handle and put it to his lips to drink. The social worker smiled at me, reassuringly.

"He can't follow simple instructions," she explained to me. "But that's okay. He'll catch back up in nursery school."

It was a disappointment for Tonino. In a cup just like that one, every afternoon, Mario and I used to pour just a drop of espresso from the little coffee pot, and then we'd fill the cup with water. That way, he didn't feel left out when we drank our coffee. Now the social worker was happy: Tonino had caught back up at school. He had learned to do what people expected him to do. After class, he'd come back home and run into his father's room. He'd climb up on the mattress, turn the sheets into a tent. He'd hide under the bed, playing hide and seek, and Mario, who was too weak even to talk, would stretch out his arm and knock on the side of the bed. That was the signal, Tonino knew: his hiding place had been found.

Once in a while he'd ask me to give him my tools so that he could give Mario a manicure. "Listen to Mamma, be careful," but I actually knew that Tonino used the nail file with a precision and patience that even I no longer had, not since my hands started shaking: with crayons and a coloring book, he'd always scribble outside the line, but he had never gotten nail polish on a cuticle.

That's how Mario and I met: I'd given him a manicure the morning of his wedding.

And so now, even if Mario was barely conscious, I let Tonino do his nails.

While Tonino was absorbing my profession, I was inheriting Mario's. Not with his responsibilities, not with his salary. I could deal drugs, though: other women did it. The women on the ground floor just sat at their doorways until a certain hour every day, like tellers at a bank window. But I lived on the eighth floor, and I had to go all the way downstairs and into the street. Still, out on the outskirts of town, the hours were pretty convenient: from 6:30 until midnight, one in the morning at the latest. I'd leave Tonino in front of the television and find him asleep. Until the end of November, it wasn't cold, December was harder, but in December my neighbor set up a fireworks stall on the street; we lit a fire in a metal drum, we bundled the kids up in overcoats, and we kept them with us until late.

Tonino was at school when Mario died. I called the social worker.

"You have to keep him."

"Where am I supposed to keep him?"

"I don't know: but you keep him until we've got Mario in the ground."

Thirty-six hours later, Tonino came home and walked straight into the bedroom without even putting down his book bag. I closed the front door; then I turned and saw him, sitting on the floor, knocking on the side of the bed.

*

Roberto had showed up just as the funeral procession was rounding the corner outside the church. But at the cemetery, when everyone came over to speak to me, I didn't see him. He showed up again for the thirtieth-day requiem, listened to the entire Mass, and then saw me home.

"Is there anything I can do to help you?"

"Do you have family?"

"I have a sister; she's a concierge in Via Toledo, just a few doors up from my business."

"Does she have children?"

"Yes, two boys."

"Could you take Tonino over there, in the afternoons, just to distract him? He could play with your nephews . . ."

He'd bring him back to me at eight o'clock. I told him I'd come downstairs to wait for him outside the gate: of all people, I didn't want Roberto to see me dealing drugs. In the end, though, I'm pretty sure that he knew. In my way, I thanked him for having left that matter in doubt. "Listen, Roberto, it's ridiculous for us to keep using the formal when we speak, it's a charade, nobody believes in it anymore."

"Hey, what's the special occasion? Are we celebrating our first anniversary?"

At first I thought he was only kidding me, but it was around June sometime when he said that. And it was on Saint Anthony's Day—June 13—that Mario last looked at the awning of this pharmacy with his own eyes. I think back on it now, but at the time I couldn't have said how long Roberto and I had known one another, and this difference between his memory of the passing days and my own, if I'd only understood, would have made it less of a surprise when he asked me to marry him. I knew right away he was interested in me, but marriage is another matter, and we had embraced only once, outside of the President movie theater, because I hadn't sat down in a movie theater since Tonino was born.

But he wasn't stupid: he wasn't encouraged by my feelings, he was encouraged by the fact that I had no choice.

And it wasn't a question of having a choice. It's that, if you marry a man sooner or later you have to go to bed with him, and then it's not just telling him thanks for doing you that favor nobody asked him for. Sooner or later, the day comes when you fight, when you're tired, and you find yourself saying something you shouldn't have, even if the terms of the deal are that you got married to live in peace.

And that's when I remembered the times when my nerves were shot, and Mario would come home and flop down onto the unmade bed in his work clothes, and Tonino had been out of control for hours, and maybe he hadn't even have taken a nap in the afternoon, hadn't slept for a minute, and I was behind with the housework, and I wished I could have had a hot meal ready for him, but the water wasn't even boiling yet, and then Capisante might call him, and Mario would say: "I have to go out again in half an hour," even when it was ten at night. And then I would start screaming and I'd get angry and throw a plate at him, and he would curse my mother, who had made me the way I was, and he'd come very close to hitting me. Then, later on, when I'd calm my nerves by rinsing the salad, little by little I'd stop ripping at the lettuce leaves, and suddenly I'd turn around: and there would be Mario, looking at me. He might already have been looking at me for a minute or so, and I hadn't even noticed. Times like that made me feel so beautiful, even if I was sweaty and tired. Maybe I felt beautiful because I was sweaty and tired on his account: I felt my breasts swelling inside my dress with every breath I took, and my legs trembling until he came over to calm them.

"Roberto, there's nothing but crust and crumbs here; there's no proper bread for you."

That's how I put it to him the next morning, at the front door of the apartment building, then I stroked his cheek and went back upstairs: because I had come down wearing slippers, and I didn't like the other tenants to see me.

Used to be there was only one road that ran from Gianturco to here. To get to Piazza Garibaldi, you had to leave yourself a good hour, with all the traffic and the gridlock. No one ever left themselves an hour: we thought that road was much shorter than the time it really took. But ever since they built the new thoroughfare, you can see who is coming, practically from your front door: our customers would arrive on motorbikes, or by bus. They'd get out at the bus stop on the bridge, walk down the curve, along the guardrail. Smiles broke out on their faces under the orange streetlamps.

"Two fifties," said one of the pair, and I should have figured it out for myself: if he hadn't already sold his gold bracelet there had to be a reason.

"Wait there," I said, and I turned around, walking over to the trash can. While I was reaching down for the fifty-thousand-lire baggies, I was still far enough away to run. I could have gotten to the parked car, and then peeled out of there. Come back inside, take Staircase C, walk across the terrace, and make it back into the apartment. And once I was inside, there was no fucking way just two of them would come looking for me.

In the apartment, I would have found Tonino's half-eaten meal, Tonino in front of the television set. I would have worried about it later, sitting on the balcony, with my neighbor: "This kid just isn't eating," I would have said, dangling one foot, bouncing my flipflop on my big toe.

But it had been two years now: nearly every evening I walked over to that trash can, ever since the city commissioner had installed the new urban furnishings. They had pulled up in trucks, when we still had cesspools instead of sewer lines, and if it rained for three days in a row, the filth would overflow, and we couldn't send the children to school. And they had unloaded a hundred red plastic vases. The civil engineer who was measuring the distance from one vase to the next explained to us that they had been designed, especially for us, by a famous architect in Milan, who had also done work on the Public Gardens. As soon as they left, the kids started knocking them over, using staves they'd ripped off of the benches as clubs. My neighbor carefully removed one and took it back to her apartment to use as a laundry hamper. Then, that evening, Capisante came by. He walked around one of the big red drums, and then spread the word not to destroy them.

Ever since then, I had been fishing twenty-four-thousand-lire heroin baggies and fifty-thousand-lire cocaine baggies out of that can. They were tiny pouches that weighed much less than a half gram, and there were periods when there was practically no good shit at all in them, but even so, nobody complained much, or if they did, I didn't hear about it. I walked that accustomed route on autopilot, without thinking. More importantly, I walked back, with the drugs, and with both feet pointing directly at the two undercover detectives, because I was tired, and when I'm tired I prefer to believe that everything is fine.

I didn't say it because I was looking for an answer. I said it because it was the only thought tormenting me, as I climbed into the police car, and because the policewoman was the first woman I saw: "I have an eight-year-old boy, upstairs, and he has no one but me."

"Then what are you doing down here in the street?"

It's something we need to take into account. We take it into account so seriously, that we aren't frightened, and that's the real challenge: to keep from being afraid. We know more or less what to say, we definitely know what not to say, who to wait for, what to ask for. The history and daily life of our quarter is so bound up with people going to prison and getting out of prison that I have never heard anyone say, to save face, to cover up their shame or embarrassment, that they were away for work, doing long-distance truck-driving, or working on a freighter, or that they had been sick, really sick, and in the hospital for the past few months. Prison doesn't isolate, it brings us together. Seeing them come home from prison is like meeting up after the end of a war, telling stories to get over it, or saying nothing, so as not to think back on it. When Capisante's brother-in-law finished his house arrest, they shot off fireworks at two in the morning from the main piazza. For men, it's a major rite of passage: survive prison and you're someone special, the bosses know that they can trust you, that they can give you bigger jobs, bigger responsibilities.

It's not the same for a woman. Unless you're planning to become a boss yourself, and there aren't many female bosses, for a woman the only possibility, the only training is to keep from ever thinking about it. You have to get used to not thinking about certain things. Tonino isn't an overbearing child, but he's no fool, either. And this middle way has always been a problem in our neighborhood. Tonino defends himself without reacting: he falls silent. When Mario and I would have fights in front of him, or when I yell at him, or when the social worker asks him a question to make him think about something he doesn't want to think about, Tonino looks out the window, or if there's no window, he looks at the floor or the ground, but beyond the floor, into the distance. Distant from me, from himself, from everyone. And when he looks into that distance, there is nothing you can do, no way to reach him. That was it: I needed to avoid thinking about Tonino, locked up in an institution, looking into the distance. I needed to keep from thinking about that. That's what surviving two years in prison is. The only known way to survive.

But what I wasn't thinking about, I was losing.

I used to go do waxing for certain ladies whose children were out of Italy. They had left the country, and were studying in America, or they were working on research projects, and they were gone for years. They would call home, maybe every other week, for a short phone conversation, a few minutes of words that they could hardly even hear.

"First and foremost, I am a mother," they kept saying. But it was bullshit. I think they liked to listen to themselves repeating those words in their minds, and they liked to hear themselves saying them out loud, but I knew from the start that those were empty words: motherhood ends if they take it away from you, if every time that you think about it you have to push it back under in order to survive.

One day, I had a son, and another day, someone decided that it was no longer my job to raise him, that I am more at fault with the rest of the world if I stay on the outside than with Tonino if I wind up in prison, and so I am no longer a mother, as those women used to put it. I had a responsibility, which I could only accept by living. It's not that I lived well, I made mistakes, I lived badly, very badly, but the only way I knew how to accept that responsibility was to make myself responsible for living. In jail, all that was left to me was the weight of responsibility. And even if I had been innocent, even if I hadn't handed over baggies of cocaine to the police that day, even then the guilt would have grown all the time that I was in prison, for every minute that Tonino wondered where I was, or learned to stop wondering where I was.

When I was awake, I managed pretty well: I would walk around in my cell, measuring the space with my body, but with time, that stopped working. We were each our body at age thirteen, when we couldn't sleep belly-down because our mammary glands were demanding to grow, and then every month for all the years allowed to us. My body was Tonino's time and space; the hours: the interval between two breast-feedings. But prison isn't a punishment of the soul for a soul that has erred, as the parish priest tried to tell us at Mass. It is the punishment of the body for a body that didn't know how to do things any other way. Still, as long as I was awake I managed to keep my mind off of it: I would stand on tiptoes and tell about my last plunging necklines before winding up in this cell, and I had discovered a method for filing my nails on the stone walls. Then, one night, I dreamt that I was being strangled with an umbilical cord, and without a balcony to take a deep breath and tell myself that I was dreaming, that fear became the only reality. It was Luisa who called the guards, because she had spent the whole day suffering from the scar on her leg, and now she wanted to go to sleep. I started taking pills: high heels are forbidden in prison, but you can have all the sleep therapies you want. And I started seeing a psychologist.

She explained my anguish as the product of the damage that prison had made part of my life: she listed the damages, lay them out for me, and then told me that they were were few in number, and that I could overcome them all, but she was wrong about me. That wasn't the problem, because I was experiencing that kind of damage even when I was on the outside, a free woman: already life had forced me to give up putting my son to bed every evening. Already I had been deprived of that choice, and I was ashamed even while I was doing things in the only way I knew how. To that extent, prison was nothing new for me.

The only thing was that I began to feel an anxiety deep inside. It was my soul, running frantically inside a body confined in a space four yards by three: as if, while I was standing still, doing nothing, there was someone in my head, running in my place, growing increasingly frantic, and never getting anywhere. But where she was trying to go, I still can't say. The psychologist said that this was normal, that this anxiety of mine, just like the depressions other women experienced, are the two most common ways of trying to escape the present.

When she told me that, I looked at my present and I knew what she meant. I *knew* what she had only understood, but it irritated me to have to stand there and confirm it.

"Once you're out, little by little you'll slow down, and one day, when you're not thinking about it anymore, you'll stop running without even realizing it."

"All right," I said.

They gave us colored plastic beads and fine black cotton strings, and told us to make bracelets. The first one I made I gave to Tonino as soon as I saw him in the recreation area. I tied three knots, tight around his wrist, and I told him never to take it off. The next week, he was back, without the bracelet.

"Can you make me another one? I gave it to my teacher."

"Why did you do that?"

"Because it was the most beautiful thing I had."

It was his last year in elementary school. I tried to imagine, at the other end of the bracelet, his teacher, and I wondered whether she had ever tried to imagine me. We made hundreds of bracelets for Christmas, and we all traded them for cigarettes. For my last Christmas in prison, I made a manger scene in the common room, and I had my picture taken lying in front of it, makeup applied with great care.

"Make the shot tight, close in," I had said to Luisa.

But Luisa didn't make it tight enough and when I look at the photograph now, I have to put my thumb on the right margin to cover the bit of prison bars that you can see behind the castle of the Three Kings.

On December 31, a postcard arrived from Roberto. It was a picture of Via Toledo, from when carriages still clip-clopped along it. On the back was written *325* in great big letters in the middle, and under that, *Buon Anno, Roberto*.

Roberto had done his math: this was the beginning of my year of work-release, and he thought that for a few hours every day, I would be able to go where I wanted. But that wasn't how it was: I worked every day in a cooperative from eight till three, then it was back to prison. Tonino was in a boarding school that was a two-hour drive away from me, and so every so often he would run away, make his way to the bus stop, board one without a ticket, and the ticket checkers—when they saw how tall he was—refused to believe that he was only eleven. I couldn't tell him not to do it anymore.

"See if you can finish this school without getting in too much trouble, Tonino."

"But I want to be a beautician."

"After you finish middle school we'll see."

"No, ma, what do you mean we'll see? I want to go to beautician's school."

One afternoon, the buses weren't running, and Tonino spent the night in the cooperative. The cooperative staff called the principal of the boarding school to reassure him, and he said that things couldn't go on like this.

Walking into the cooperative at eight in the morning and finding Tonino eating breakfast and chatting with the others was a real morning after such a long time.

Once Tonino was on his way back, they told me to call the principal.

"Signora, I have to see you as soon as possible."

"Principal, you have the address of the women's

prison. I receive visitors on Saturday after three in the afternoon."

Instead, I wound up going to see him: on a special furlough, with two plainclothes guards accompanying me one Sunday to the boarding school; they left me there and told me that they'd go to the main train station at three that afternoon to pick me up. I was going to surprise Tonino.

Once the car door had slammed, I was left alone outside the boarding school's garden. Here I was: I could go in. Or sit down on the low wall and smoke a cigarette. Or walk along the trolley tracks all the way to the beach. I felt like Luisa, the first day she walked without crutches on her stabbed leg; I felt like Tonino the night that I didn't come home.

I walked in. I spoke to the principal, I told him that I didn't have long to serve: a year isn't long. That I had started a countdown: "And you can start a countdown of your own: Tonino is going to take the final exam and then he'll never set foot in here again."

"Signora, don't take me wrong, but as long as he's here, he has to study like the others and respect certain rules."

"What if, in order to study like the others, he has to break certain rules every once in a while?"

I left him thinking that one over, and I went to see Tonino, in the chapel where they were all attending Sunday Mass. As I walked in, the priest was holding up the wafer, and Tonino was brushing a lock of hair from his eyes. As he did, the nun kneeling behind him grabbed his arm and gave it a sharp tug. I dipped my finger in holy water, crossed myself, and walked over to the nun: "Step outside."

"Shhh."

"Don't be ridiculous: step outside."

"But, pardon me, what is this about?"

I seized her by the arm and hauled her to her feet; she understood and followed me outside.

"You're that boy's mother."

"Hmm."

"Dear Signora, I'm doing it for your son's own good; don't you see that he's effeminate?"

"Right, and so you have the right to mistreat him, because he fiddles with his hair; help me understand that one . . ."

"That boy plucks his eyebrows with a pair of tweezers."

"He can take it up the ass for all I care, but you don't lay a finger on him, ever again. Understood?"

"No, I'm not going to go on talking like this; I won't put up with this . . ."

So I knocked her back on her heels and pinned her shoulders against the stone church wall.

"Listen, you. If you have problems with Tonino, you tell me about them. Get it? Because his father's dead, but his mother's alive and well. Got it?"

I sank my fingernails into the heavy cloth of her habit. She started trembling.

"I'm still alive. Can you tell? Can you feel that I'm still alive?"

We went out and got some fried fish, then we walked down together to the train station, long before the appointment. I had forgotten how beautiful Piazza Garibaldi is, with the kebab stand on the corner by the pharmacy, and all the street vendors along the Vicolo della Duchesca.

We walked along the sidewalk lined with banks, Tonino

bought a pair of sunglasses, and I bought a pair of boots with four-inch heels, but I left them in the box: "I'll wear them when I come home."

We started off toward Piazza Nolana because I wanted to take a look at the sea, even if it was just the harbor, but instead we only got as far as the church of Santa Maria del Carmine, because there was so much stuff laid out for sale on the sidewalk that it was impossible to get through. The fish market was shutting down, and the vendors were hosing down the street. The water flowed away downhill through the gate of Porta Nolana, and then I took a deep breath and asked him: "Tonino, tell Mamma, you're not a faggot, are you?"

When it was just a few weeks till my sentence was up, deep inside I was still running, and instead of slowing down, the pace only sped up: and I was flattened by the pressure against the back wall of my cell, staring at the door, as if it was the first door I'd ever seen in my life and I didn't know what it was for. Day after horrible day of terror; I stopped going to the cooperative, I stopped going outside during recreation hour.

And then, all the same, I was released.

I walk into the main entrance of number 325, Via Toledo.

Between the majolica coat of arms and the anodyzed aluminum elevator is the concierge's little booth.

I look around me; the concierge raises her head and studies me. I ignore her and let her look.

A gentleman walks in behind me, and he too looks around.

"Who are you looking for?" she asks him.

"Law firm of Nucifero."

"Third floor, on the left."

The man leaves, she steps out of her booth, and we stand facing one another. The instant I look at her I know that she resembles Roberto, by certain tangled connections of facial features, she reminds me of him. I pull out of my pocket the postcard, folded in four: I hand it to her.

She takes it and opens it. She reads the only thing that's printed on it: *house of detention*. Then she returns to her booth and gets a bucket.

"Come with me . . ."

From a door beneath the main stairs, we slip out into a series of narrow courtyards, we make our way through the belly of the apartment buildings, out toward the poorer quarters. And as we move away from the elegant commercial street, the buildings become darker, more smoke-stained: bundles of electric cables run along beside us like a handrail, when we start walking downstairs. She tells me to look at the marks in the tufa stone.

"This is where we took shelter during the bombing raids."

"How old were you, ma'am?"

"Four."

"And you remember it?"

"Signora, everything that I can remember in my life starts right here."

After four or five flights of stairs, the neon lights become too dim, I can feel the dampness in my bones, even though it's summer. We walk further along, down a straight corridor. I have the impression that we're going toward the poorer quarters, toward the hill.

"Are we going toward the Corso?"

"No: we've only crossed the street. We're underneath number 121, Via Toledo, the Banca Intesa building."

The tunnel dead-ends into a wall. The concierge starts waving hello to the wall, and I turn at the whirring sound of a surveillance camera until I see it: it tilts the lens slightly to focus on us. Now the concierge starts talking quickly, complaining at some length because her sons are all grown up but they still live at home, her laundry hamper is always overflowing, even though she runs the washing machine three times a day, every blessed day, and when they finally move out and have to pay their own bills, oh they'll understand what being wasteful means then. As she's chattering away, she thrusts objects into my arms: a garden hose, a broom. She fills the bucket with rags, she grabs a box of Ava powdered detergent. The surveillance camera swivels as we move off down the hallway. She turns around, one last time, before we turn the corner, and smiles at the camera.

"This is the safest place I know. Ever since I was four years old, every time I come down here I feel like a baby in her mother's belly. And that's why I put it here."

"What about the surveillance camera?"

"Well, across the street used to be the Motta restaurant, you remember it?"

"Of course."

"Back then, you could still take the underpass to the other side of Via Toledo, and you came up inside the building across the way. Then, when the bank moved in, they closed the underpass with a big steel plate, and then they built that wall. But, evidently, they're still worried. They must know that bad guys can get in from every direction, so they've installed a surveillance camera too. They know who I am: I use the tunnel to store things. Let's just say that if anyone tries to come down here without me, the police will be here in minutes: that's why I keep it here."

I look at the box of Ava powdered detergent and I'm sorry to see it's so damp, the cardboard puffy, as if there really was detergent in it. The concierge may have guessed what I was thinking, but she says nothing, because when we finally arrive back at her booth, we meet the young man from the café with two cups of espresso on his tray.

"Who are these from?"

"Pino, the security guard."

"Ah, well thank him from me . . ."

I stir my coffee, and the box still sits there, in the bucket, beneath the cleaning rags I look at it, I continue to look at it, but I don't reach out my hand. She has to give it to me. She finishes her coffee, then she picks it up and holds it out to me, with both hands.

I take it the way I took the mail in prison, the way I picked up Tonino at night to suckle him, like something that is there for me, something that has arrived from another world.

"What's inside?"

"Negotiable, interest-bearing treasury bonds. Twenty bonds, each worth fifteen thousand euros."

I scratch away a little bit of the crust coating the damp and swollen cardboard on the carton, and beneath it emerges Calimero, Ava's mascot, a little black bird.

"How long have you been hiding them?"

"My brother gave them to me four years ago, when he got married. He didn't think it was safe once there was someone else in the house, even if it was his own wife. Until then, he had always kept them."

"How is he?"

"He's well, God bless him."

"And you kept them, all this time, for your brother?"

"No, signora: I kept them for you, how can I say this . . . to thank you."

"What for?"

"Because you never said yes. Because you wouldn't marry him."

She puts the detergent box into a plastic shopping bag, and we step out into the street. The concierge looks over toward the bulletproof glass windows of the Banca Intesa and gestures with one hand to say: thanks, we got the coffee. Tonino is at the corner, near Onyx, waiting for me on his motorbike. His eyes are blue. The concierge looks at him, then she looks at me: "He's grown up."

I turn and leave, without saying a word in reply. We manage to make our way along the sidewalk, because construction is underway on the subway, but we drive carefully, cautiously, just grazing the bolts of silk piled on the stalls of the Chinese vendors.

I stop outside the plate glass window of the pharmacy. I need to select a good post-depilation oil. And a lotion, not too dense, for massages. The women we work for expect the finest products: all they ask of us is the superfluous, the unnecessary, and money is no object where that is concerned.

Beyond the Chicco brand baby rattles, in the reflections in the plate glass, I see myself on Via Marina, between the trees and the Loreto hospital, my image foreshortened in the distance.

Mario had heard it, too, the motorbike coming, he'd

heard it before Roberto did, heard it more clearly too. He'd recognized the message of pain that it was bringing. Many was the time that he'd carried that same message, the same way. He'd understood that they were looking for cocaine, and nothing else. They couldn't know that the proceeds from the weekend's sales were coming back to Capisante, deposited in eight different places around the city, in the form of interest-bearing treasury bonds. And Mario would have taken them to him, if only they had left him the chance.

He'd heard the motorbike coming up behind him when he was level with the last tree, he'd dropped the bag between the trunk and the wall, maybe he was hoping to go back and retrieve it after they left. In a city drowning in garbage, nobody notices a plastic shopping bag. He figured they would have sent someone experienced and reliable, say Luigi, or Peppino, who knew what to say and where to strike. He had stepped off the curb, expressionless, perhaps without even tensing his back, the way I am doing right now.

Roberto had picked up the bag while they were killing him. Then he had sat down on the ground, huddled on the curb, concealing the plastic bag and absorbing the horror. In the hospital bathroom, he had discovered his good fortune, his peril, his guilt, his dishonesty, his honesty, his doubt, and his hesitancy. Then Tonino had been placed into his arms.

If he had given the bonds to me right away, perhaps I'd never have gone to prison, or maybe I'd have wound up there sooner. Maybe he was waiting for me to say I'd marry him, so that he could bring them to me as part of a dowry, or maybe he was afraid to use them. Or he waited to forget about them so that he'd know what to do with them. The boss assumed that the killers on the motorbike had taken the money the day they stabbed him, and that's why he never asked me to give it back. I never even knew the money existed, and so nobody looked for it. And after all, for a boss that high up, the earnings of a single weekend might be enough to renovate his house, installing Versace tiles and toilet; it wasn't much more money than that. He certainly doesn't know that with his heroin I'm buying herbal masks for facials, the ones with honey: Tonino finds them easier to work with.

There's an old man in line ahead of me, and he's trying to persuade the pharmacist to give him the same pills I took for my sleep therapy in prison. He says that he can't find the prescription, but that he had it. I say they should give him the pills and not worry about it, I say that the pharmacist is taking on too much responsibility for the old man's nights, that they go to university and study for years and they still don't understand a thing. My psychologist too: she never got it right. When the anxiety finally leaves you, after all that time, you know it perfectly well. It's like taking off a pair of stiletto heels and slipping into a pair of slippers. Your foot gradually resumes its normal shape, your ankles slowly relax. After a while, you start to drag your feet along the floor, your belly shows a little more. And you know that nobody would notice you, looking like that. And you know that as long as you're wearing slippers, you won't go far. But that's where you want to stay.

SIDDHARTHA

Ferdinando says he's never seen a photoengraver with long fingernails.

"Look, you scratched the vellum again, of course. How can you do your job with that hand?"

"Ferdinando, what's my hand have to do with it? The paper's just flimsy . . ."

"The one thing you can't blame is the paper; I don't skimp on paper, and you know it. It's those fingernails of yours, like some queer . . . Throw this one out, do it over."

I'll do it over, but I won't cut my nails. I can't bring myself to. And it's my left hand, too. Because I've always been left-handed at everything, including the guitar. I've always done everything with my left hand: writing, holding a fork, playing scales. Every one of my schoolteachers would tell me to use my other hand. They'd say, "See how bad your handwriting is!" But look at me now: nobody writes anymore, we all use computers—even typing, my left hand is faster.

I had a deranged great-aunt who used to keep me and my sister at the dinner table for an extra half hour, teaching us how to hold our silverware. It drove me crazy. I cut more pulp than peel. In the end she would turn away and ask our mother, "What did you do, raise these children backwards?"

"Auntie, leave them alone, they're children, the main thing is to get them fed."

"Now, that's not true. Someday they'll sit down to dinner with important people, and those people won't care whether or not they eat."

"Or *how* they eat."

"And *that's* not true, either. People can tell in a second whether you have good table manners."

"And who are these children of mine going to have dinner with? The ambassador?"

"What do *you* know?"

My sister would really work at it, practically going hungry in the process. The scraps that she managed to get in her mouth went in at the exact angle, with just the right grip. She learned how to wrap spaghetti around her fork so that not a single strand dangled. As soon as my great-aunt left, I would grab a pear with my hand and bite into it ravenously.

For her part, Mamma never said a thing to me about my left hand, or my fingernails: she paid for the conservatory, and she made extra blood sausage for the neighbors after I passed my solfège exam—to compensate them for the torturous afternoons of listening to me practice my relentless exercises.

Then, one day, my teachers called her in for a meeting, "Signora, your son isn't keeping up in class. The way things are going, he won't be able to take the finals."

The second semester had just begun.

"Your son is trying to do too much, Signora. He has to choose."

And my mother had to make a choice, too: whether to talk to me about it or not. I was just finishing the Bach when she got home—I had calluses on my fingers from that piece. "It's much more difficult to play with the chords upside down," they told me at the conservatory, but in the end my left hand mastered the piece, and I could really play it.

I was running through the notes to relax my fingers.

"Matteo, your teachers say that you're not doing well at school."

"The Lit teacher?"

"Yes, your literature teacher *and* your science teacher. They both say they can't let you take finals."

"I'm doing all right. If they flunk *me*, they're going to have to flunk half the class."

"Listen to me, Matteo. I know that you've been working hard practicing your scales. But now you've got to focus and do your best."

"But, Mamma, it's only February; the final exams are in June."

"Matteo, they're telling me that it'll be a miracle if you can make up the work. You have both exams . . ."

"I'll work hard."

"Look. You're done with the boring part of guitar. Now comes the fun part. Why don't you quit conservatory until after the state exams? Then you can start again in September. Nothing lost. The diploma is important. What can you do these days without a high-school diploma?"

My teachers admitted me to final exams, and I scraped through with a passing grade. But I will never forgive them for having forced my mother to look at me that way, like someone who can't bear to look at you but looks anyway.

I haven't touched a guitar since then. It's been seven years, and I'm not about to start playing again, now that we're locked up in this print shop from eight in the morning till six at night. But I still won't cut my fingernails. I'm positive that if I picked up a guitar now, the music would come back to me, but all those fingering exercises that I did, now they only help me to work faster with the printing plates.

I prepare another sheet of vellum and hand it to Guglielmo for printing, telling him, "Center the little gold hearts on the fold on the coated stock."

At one o'clock, they come to pick up the wedding announcements, then we pull out a sheet of vellum paper and stretch it out carefully on the central work table, but the paper is stiff, and it shifts around, so Guglielmo picks up four Anne Franks and weighs down the corners. Then we each lay out our lunch. I hunch over my escarole pizza, and don't look up, even when someone talks to me this time of day everyone is just fooling around anyway, taking advantage of the fact that Ferdinando goes home for lunch.

"Maybe on the days when we've got a tight deadline, we should just have *colazione* like my cousin in Brescia."

"You mean just eat a sandwich?"

"No, they call it *colazione*, yogurt, a *pizzetta*, and then nothing until dinner."

We all listen to Michele, but don't believe a word he says, because while he's talking his mouth is full of the sausage and red peppers that his wife fries up for him at six in the morning, one hand clutching her belly. Poor Rosetta is pregnant, and the smell of frying at dawn makes her nauseous for the rest of the day.

"Give me a break . . . 'when we have a tight deadline.'"

Why don't you just admit your wife is sick and tired of cooking for you, so you come up with stories about your cousin in Brescia?"

"I'm not kidding: these Fabrianos are serious business, and they need to be done by the end of the day tomorrow, no later. They can't be sitting around in the warehouse for even an hour."

"Ferdinando told me that he's bringing his wife and daughter tomorrow, and we'll all work together and get it done the same day."

"Well, let's hope so . . ."

"Why are you so worried?"

"The Fabrianos are riskier than the books, because we aren't selling them to sidewalk vendors; they're going into real stationery shops, right next to the real ones."

"So?"

"It scares me, that's all."

"Michele, you're still in shock."

Michele had been in shock for the past eight months. Ever since the day that Ferdinando had come in with a Priority Mail stamp and said, "Make me a plate of this one."

I made him a plate. Then he went over to Guglielmo, who was printing fliers for the pizzeria across the street, which was going to start making home deliveries, and turned off the press without a word.

He handed him the plate for the Priority Mail stamp, and said, "Run off four thousand of these, eighty per sheet."

Guglielmo took the plate and looked at it carefully, he even held it up to the light, and then looked Ferdinando in the eye and said, "Don Ferdinando, I'm not printing these."

"Why not?"

"I'm scared to. These aren't Anne Franks, you know . . ."

Ferdinando smiled at him, and gripped his forearm like a father. "Guglielmo, I'll take responsibility."

"Don Ferdinando: if the Postmaster General calls me into his office and *he* tells me, 'I'll take responsibility,' then I'll print them."

So Ferdinando went over to Michele and offered him some money.

Just a few evenings before, Rosetta took Michele aside when he'd come home and said, "Darling, we're going to have a baby," and since Michele really cared about the *we* and had spent the whole night thinking it over while Rosetta slept beside him—well, that infamous Tuesday afternoon, Michele answered, "Sure, Ferdinando, no problem, but we do it after work, when the shop is closed."

Then he called Rosetta, holding the Priority Mail stamp in one hand, and told her, "I'm working late tonight," and Rosetta must have been angry about that, but Michele could hardly explain.

As soon as we left that day, Michele and Ferdinando began printing, and they had almost finished when a treasury agent began pounding on the metal shutter in the front of the shop, and another one came in through the courtyard door that they left open because of the stink from the water we used to clean the rollers.

A guy who owned a local tobacco shop couldn't get the idea out of his head that he'd been left out of the deal, so he called in an anonymous tip. "A printing shop in a cross street along the row houses at San Rocco." The agents had driven up and down the main road until they finally found the place.

It was Michele's good luck that, just when the police raided the shop, he was in the back, talking to Rosetta on the phone, because she had suddenly sensed that the baby was a boy, and had called, breathless, to tell him. But they caught Ferdinando with the fake Priority Mail stamps in his hands, and arrested him on the spot.

From Poggioreale prison, Ferdinando wrote me a letter that started like this: We were all one big family, and he loved me like a son, and that of all his sons I was the only one who knew how to string two words together. He asked me to speak with the lawyer, and then he wrote a few other things in code, but I understood exactly what he wanted: the fake accounting records needed to disappear. When the letter arrived, it made me feel pretty bad, because we'd never had a letter delivered to our house from anyone in prison before. I stayed up all night talking it over with my sister, and we finally decided not to say anything to our mother.

Ferdinando didn't do well in prison. He turned anorexic, so after a month they gave him house arrest. But even at home Ferdinando was depressed; his relatives wouldn't forgive him: having the head of the household sitting in the easy chair dressed in his pajamas was ruining their Sunday dinners. On Christmas Eve, when they called him to lead the blessing at dinner, he just couldn't do it.

"Gracious, Ferdinando," said his wife. "Come on, cheer up, it's just another two months."

"Really, Papa, you've been like this ever since they let you out."

"Hey, Grandpa, when are they going to put you back in jail?" asked his granddaughter, bringing up the rear.

From then on, we never did anything that was really, dangerously, illegal in the print shop.

At seven o'clock, I hop on my scooter, drop Michele off at the subway, and then ride the length of the Frullone to our apartment.

At home, I find my sister flopped over her books and Mamma in the bathroom. I knock on the door to let her know I'm home, and I hear a flush—she was sneaking a smoke. Whenever she hears me or Daniela coming toward the bathroom, she runs the cigarette under the faucet to put it out, wraps it in toilet paper, and flushes. Then she spends two more minutes in the bathroom with the window open, brushing her teeth and, if it's really necessary, she sprays the window shade with the first bottle of perfume she can lay her hands on.

"Hey," she says to me.

"Hey," I respond.

"Dinner'll be ready in half an hour."

I go into my bedroom, stinking to high heaven from the kerosene that we use to clean the plates after each print run, and then I come back out with clean clothes under one arm, dying for a shower. The bathroom stinks like tobacco and White Musk.

"Tell Daniela dinner's ready," Mamma shouts, in the seven hundred and fifty square feet of our apartment, so loud that Daniela can hear it just as well as I can—but since Daniela's studying for an exam, she doesn't want to be disturbed.

"Daniela, dinner's ready," I shout, just as loud as Mamma.

Daniela sits down at the dinner table wearing pajamas that she hasn't taken off in three days, a pair of socks, and a headband that I gave her in the eighties. She barely acknowledges my presence, and hands me a sheet of paper. "See if you can get me a copy," she says.

I read: *History of the Kingdom of Naples,* by Benedetto Croce. I shake my head. We have lots of books about Naples: *The Proverbs, The Neapolitan-Italian Dictionary,* and even *Neapolitan Cooking* by Caròla-Francesconi, which Mamma uses as a trivet for her pots and pans since she always cooks the same things.

"When did you stop doing university textbooks?"

"Mamma, we never did university textbooks. We only copy books that lots of people want to buy."

The confusion in my mother's head dates back to when Daniela was studying advanced Italian literature and we happened at the same time to get not only the plates for Pavese's *The Moon and the Bonfires* but even the same paper that the original publisher had used, purchased from the same distributor.

Ferdinando can say what he wants about my fingernails, but with a clean original, and good paper, we produced a book that—forget about sidewalk vendors—you could have passed that book off on the author himself.

Daniela took the exam and passed with honors. And there were a few other times, if he happened to have a pile of books from Newton & Compton, when he would give me a few. In the end, Ferdinando would always tell me— partly because he loves me, partly because he never did the paperwork to make me legal—"Matteo, since your sister is studying for her exams, you take what you want."

Mamma won't give it up. "*History of the Kingdom of Naples* doesn't sell?"

"I don't know, but they only ask us to print the ones

that really sell a lot. The ones that always sell: *The Diary of Anne Frank*, *Siddhartha*, *Catcher in the Rye*."

"I've read them."

"I know."

"One of them, I don't know which, was missing ten pages in the middle."

"That was Guglielmo: when there are pages missing, it's Guglielmo, because Michele is careful."

"How is his wife?"

"I think she's fine."

"What month is she?"

"Still in her eighth month—just like two days ago, the last time you asked."

"Are you in a bad mood?"

Finally Daniela snaps out of it and comes to my rescue. "Mamma, he's tired."

"Are you tired?"

"This morning I printed wedding invitations and this afternoon holy cards for a memorial service . . . they wanted a picture of the dead man, and peeping out from behind him, sort of in filigree, the face of Padre Pio. We had to finish everything by tonight, because tomorrow we're doing the Fabrianos."

Mamma gets up and starts clearing the table, and Daniela pulls me outside, onto the balcony. She turns off the light.

"Light a cigarette and let me have a couple of puffs."

I hand it to her.

"When is your exam?"

"The day after tomorrow. I have to study all night."

"Just don't wear yourself out."

"I'll take a nap."

And she takes a cigarette from my packet while she's at it, for later tonight. Because Daniela sneaks cigarettes too, out on the balcony, when Mamma goes downstairs to buy groceries or to have coffee with the neighbor. She leaves the door open to hear if Mamma comes back in, and smokes, pressed up against the wall on the balcony like a lizard. She digs a little hole in the soil in the potted plants, and taps the ashes into it, then tosses the butt down into the courtyard.

Mamma knows, just like Daniela knows that Mamma smokes in the bathroom, but neither one of them wants to disappoint the other.

As I'm getting ready to go to bed, Mamma stops me at the door of my bedroom. "Listen."

"What?"

"When is your sister's exam?"

"Who knows?"

First thing in the morning, when I get to the print shop, the whole family is there, manning the assembly line. Ferdinando's daughter runs the sheets through the paper cutter, his wife glues the four heavy cardboard corners to the base, and his niece fills the holder with paper. Instead of ten sheets per album, she is supposed to put nine. Ferdinando is all excited: he is pulling the A1 sheets out of the packing paper with his arms straight out, as if he were folding linen, and he sniffs the paper; he lets me touch a corner of one sheet and says, "Look at it, Matteo, look at how pretty it is."

And the paper really is pretty. This paper comes from the Fabriano paper mills with untrimmed edges, like sheets of dowry linen. Before they'd delivered them to us, the truck had taken the paper by Peppe lo Scalzo's shop, and he'd stamped them with an "F" for Fabriano.

If we keep working this fast, we'll be done by lunchtime, and in fact, at two o'clock, Ferdinando's wife pulls out four nice macaroni frittatas and says, "Be my guests." Then they clear up and leave, and it's just us men, packing the finished goods.

While we are still taping shut the last packets, the truck that's going to deliver them to the stationery shops pulls up. Michele heaves a big sigh of relief, and then his cell phone goes off, with Rosetta's ring tone. So, with seven packets of Fabriano's in his arms, he goes to answer, and trips over an Anne Frank.

"Bloody hell," he says, "that girl is always underfoot."

Then, we watch as he turns beet-red and seems to swell up, growing larger and larger as he speaks, until, by the time he stands up, he looks like he's six-and-a-half feet tall, and bursting out of his clothes.

"Rosetta had a contraction," he says, then suddenly looking at us, "It's not dangerous to give birth at eight months, is it?"

Ferdinando, Guglielmo, the truck driver, and I all say, "No-o-o," in unison and we even shake our heads vigorously. In reality, of course, none of us has the slightest idea.

"Go on, go home," Ferdinando sends him off with a gesture of benediction, and I say to him, "You can take my scooter."

And so we all step out of the front door of the print shop, and we watch this lovely little vignette, with the truck roaring off, loaded with packages of Fabrianos, and behind the truck, Michele, tearing along as fast as he can go, keeping pace with the truck, riding my little scooter, which makes him look like the Incredible Hulk. And as we watch them turn off the boulevard toward the Frullone, we see, coming from the opposite direction, cars full of treasury agents.

"I would like to know how this baby knows," Ferdinando says, "how he always knows when it's time to call his father."

But he's not really worried, because the shop is clean, and so when the chief officer says, "Inspection," we all look at him with big, easy smiles on our faces.

And in fact, all the documents are in order; I am the only one in the shop who is working under the counter, because Ferdinando never had time for the paperwork to hire me officially, but the officer looks at me and says, "I bet you're still on probation."

"Umm," I say.

"Mmm," he replies, "well, let's go ahead and request the document check, just an hour or so, and then we all go home. But, do me a favor please, and turn off your cell phones."

"Rats," I say, "I wanted to ask my mother if it's dangerous to give birth at eight months."

The officer looks at me funny, as if it were a coded message, and so we explain the whole story to him, and he relaxes; he tells us that his wife gave birth at eight months, too, and now his son is a big boy, a handsome eleven-year old who, just the other day, learned how to assemble his police-issue pistol.

So, what with one thing and another, between one cigarette and the next, we have an hour to kill. Ferdinando goes out into the street with the officer, and they start pointing toward the subway station, remembering when there was a farm right there.

I pull a copy of *Siddhartha* out from under the monitor, and I start reading. It's well made, the cover is centered, the paper is good.

"There are no belly bands," Guglielmo says.

"What do you want for three euros?"

Ten minutes and ten games of solitaire later, he interrupts me. "What are you doing? Are you reading it?"

"Mmm."

On page 38 he breaks in again, "How is it?"

"So-so."

"What does 'Siddhartha' mean?"

"That's his name."

Then, suddenly, I lose my temper. "What the fuck, Guglielmo, there are ten pages missing."

"It must be just this copy."

"No, the same thing happened to my mother's copy. How the fuck do you do things? How many copies did we run of this one?"

"A thousand."

"What the fuck."

"You can still read it."

"What do you mean, I can read it. This guy is always doing something new."

"You got this far, where are you? See? Page 78. You're on page 78, and you can't figure it out?"

"I guess I must be an idiot."

"What's happened so far?"

"This guy is in India, and he's the son of a rich guy, but he's not happy."

"What's the matter?"

"Nothing, he's sad, so he leaves it all behind and goes off with a friend on a trip, and he meets certain folks, and as he meets them, he starts doing the same thing that they are doing. And that's as far as I've gotten."

"Now he'll get a girlfriend."

"Don't be ridiculous."

"Sorry, go on and read what happens next."

"You've made me lose interest."

"If you ask me, he gets a girlfriend. And goes into business for himself."

I throw the book at his head and I walk out to the front door; I say to the treasury agent, "Officer, do me a favor. Could you arrest that guy and take him away? Please."

"Do you have a cigarette?" he replies.

"Sure, let's have a smoke," and I reach out my hand to pass him my pack.

He looks at my fingernails. "You play the guitar?"

"I stopped."

"When are you going to start playing again?" he asks, and hands me a box of matches.

I light up, and as I do I feel an idea coming into my head that has nothing to do with me right now, something that comes from the past or the future.

And yet, I feel certain when I answer him, "Soon."

THE IMAGINED FRIEND

1.

It vibrated three times in her handbag. So Marina got ready.

Smiling but without explanation, she moved a few steps away from the group, walking a short way along the western wing of the patio, and then stopped at the foot of the second column. As she pulled her cell phone out of her purse, she noticed that nightfall was darkening the museum, and saw a white dot reflected in the window of the Sala Farnese, and she sensed that Vesper the Evening Star, together with that message from Ernesto, made her life perfect.

When she rejoined the group, the others told her that Biagio had arrived, with Agnese, and that with her hair cut short her daughter looked remarkably like her. She searched the hall for them, and found Biagio in front of "Sheep in Formaldehyde", doing his best to persuade the little girl that it was just a statue.

Biagio smiled at her as he saw her coming toward them, and gestured with one hand, behind Agnese's head: things were getting sticky.

"More than contemporary art it seems like a natural history museum . . ."

"Where the scientists overdo it with the formalde-hyde . . ."

The child didn't even greet her mother, rapt in her contemplation of the decomposing artworks. Marina pointed to Agnese and spoke to her husband: "She's not the only one the work has had this effect on."

"Who else?"

"The artist himself: he said: 'Some of my creations are silly and embarrassing . . .'"

Wrapped in the arm of her husband, which was perfectly shaped, with ideal height and angle, Marina strolled back toward the *Horse Carcass* while describing her day to him, point by point, beginning with the demonstration of the jobless activists of Available Labor Force. Beginning with the unemployed protester who managed, with the connivance of the attendant from the service court, to climb up to the storage floor, where he walked past the dust-covered artifacts, amphorae, capitals, crates filled with glass pieces—might even have pilfered something—and then swung open one of the museum windows that hadn't been opened in either of their lifetimes, and had stepped up and out, looking down over the city.

And from a vast cornice, so broad that it seemed the bridge of a ship, he had bawled: "I'LL JUMP! PROFESSIONAL RETRAINING, OR I'LL JUMP!"

"Agnese talks to herself . . ."

"No, she's not talking to herself," Marina explained to Dottoressa Donati, swallowing that sharp barb of pain that she always felt when she had to make excuses for Agnese to someone who was no one—a colleague, an acquaintance.

"She's not talking to herself: she has an imaginary friend."

"Who is it?"

"I've never seen him . . ."

"C'mon, what I mean is . . . is it a cartoon character?"

"No, no: she invented him all by herself. She calls him Daniele."

"I would have expected something more exotic . . . something like *Horatio*."

"No, not at all. *Daniele*."

Marina watched as Agnese moved through the festive crowd far more smoothly than the representatives of the local press, describing everything she saw loudly. She crossed the courtyard and leaned over to explain to her that the artworks weren't actually made with real animals.

"Mamma says that they're puppets," Agnese told her imaginary friend.

The inauguration concluded with a dinner in the Hall of the Sundial. Invitations strictly reserved for gallery owners and artists, with a city commissioner at the door, who couldn't accept the idea of just going for a bite in a trattoria. The regional governor had made his escape earlier in the day: at a press conference he had sung the praises of the two major exhibits now open in the city, impetuously gliding over the four centuries of history that separated the two bodies of artwork, a hurtling leap from the late Cinquecento to the present day, but there was no interpreter, and the Brits hadn't understood a thing. Marina was at once slightly irritated and somewhat pleased to continue wearing, for a few hours longer, the see-through rust-colored blouse and the tango pumps, so much better suited to walking up that monumental staircase than the rubber-soled walking shoes worn by tourists.

Biagio and the girl had gone home, and she had watched them go—a little piece of her tearing away with them as they went—before being engulfed again by her duties as a press liaison, as Dodi took her by the arm and told her she absolutely must go take a look at the new gallery, that a new German artist would be coming at the beginning of the week.

This was the kind of conversation that cried out for Ernesto; he absolutely had to be told every detail at the earliest opportunity. As soon as the diners had moved on from the tagliolini timbale to the *tubetti* with clams and mussels, Marina would excuse herself from table, cross the vast hall shrouded in the penumbra that catering seemed to demand, and walking the length of the groove of the sundial, reach the open French doors.

While the sirocco knotted the Italian tricolor around the banner of Available Labor Force, she could finally call him and tell him everything. Give the proper response to the message that anyone else might have misunderstood, but not her. She knew that I can't stand the fact that I'm not there was prompted precisely by Ernesto's basic nature: the fact that he was like a chatty neighbor, the fact that he was a born gossip, a lover of juicy details, the same qualities that made him the best press officer for the finest contemporary art museum in Italy. As well as the toughest to manage of all her friends.

"Tell me *everything*."

"I'm not even going to tell you who's seated at my table."

"Why not? . . . How can you be so cruel?"

"You could have come, you know . . ."

"I'm stuck in this hellish art fair. But I'll come next week, and we'll go everywhere together . . . Who's at your table?"

"Dodi."

"Good lord, maybe the fair isn't so bad . . ."

"Brits always amaze me."

"Me too, but what, specifically?"

"They wear these black jackets three sizes too small, their cuffs stick out at least eight inches, they wear tiny neckties that are tighter than a hangman's noose, and they're incredibly elegant, but why?"

"Well, on the other hand, the British press agents all wear braided loafers . . ."

"Everyone has what they deserve . . ."

"*No one* deserves braided loafers. What about La Sabelli?"

"She showed up in a fur coat."

"So? The personal show is a collection of dead animals . . ."

"Hello? We're in the *south of Italy*. Think! Unless you're stuck on an Alp, like you are, it's *springtime*, next weekend I'm going to *Procida* . . ."

"Got it, got it, what about that monster Fabiana? What's she wearing?"

"I can't quite see her . . ."

"You must have cataracts . . ."

"We're dining by candlelight, it's dark . . ."

"You don't have electric light yet, down there in the Kingdom of Naples?"

"It's one thing that Donati can't understand it. After all, she does PR for an art gallery, but the fact that you, a doctor, are worrying about it seems concerning to me," Marina said to Biagio. Then she carried the flat wooden plates into the kitchen and handed them to Luisa, who was preparing the sushi.

"You have to just put it out of your mind that our husbands are doctors. They're moguls now, they've become power-mongers, they don't know anything about patients anymore."

"When I married him, Biagio told me: 'I don't treat a disease, I treat a person.'"

"Now they don't even treat the diseases, they just hold conferences about them."

"Anyway, do you think Agnese is strange?"

"Why did she insist on having an extra chair at the table?"

"That's not all: she gets rained on because she has to share the umbrella, she's never alone."

"Lucky thing . . ."

"My earliest memory of a comic strip was *Barnaby*, it was a little album that my father brought me from the United States . . . You know when you read a comic strip so many times that you know every panel by heart and then you keep on reading them, but in your memory?"

"Mmm."

"It was a little boy who had an imaginary friend, a 'fairy godfather' with pink wings, and all of the kid characters could see him, and only the boy's parents worried about it . . . I think it's something like that."

"Do you still have this comic strip? Maybe, if you can find it, you could give it to Agnese."

"It was in English."

"So you can read it to her."

"You know what it really is?" Marina said, coming to a stop in the hallway, holding full plates in both hands. "It's this: Biagio isn't really worried about Agnese, he's just afraid he'll look stupid in front of the others."

Luisa made a dubious grimace, the face you make when you've just heard something unpleasant. For the rest of the meal she kept Agnese occupied, teaching her to eat with chopsticks. It was not until the girl was sleeping on the couch that the conversation resumed.

"Anyway, even when Agnese is talking with *Daniele*, she knows that he doesn't exist."

"Partly she knows, and partly she's just trying to protect him, to shield him from our eyes, because if we could see him too, we'd ruin him."

"Well, females, little girls, are more prone to this sort of thing."

"Imaginary friends?"

"Imagining in general. Situations, roles, friends: and of course they're easier than real relationships, you don't have to take the time to explain how the game works, you can always be right, there're no disappointments . . ."

"If she's waiting to have non-disappointing relationships, she'll turn into a little old lady, poor thing," said Marina, as she got up to make coffee.

press@castello.it
you in the office?
Ernesto

marina@lagalleria.it
Yes, want to talk?

press@castello.it
Later: right now, Christian is fifteen feet away from me, and
I wanted to tell you some mean things about Christian
E.

> marina@lagalleria.it
> is that the guy who always wears Converse All-Stars,
> even when it's fifteen below zero? Then why don't
> you write mean things about Christian to me, while
> he's fifteen feet away . . . isn't that even better?
> What are you doing this w. end?

press@castello.it
I'm going to a soccer game with Christian
E.

> marina@lagalleria.it
> The whole w. end?

press@castello.it
That's the MAIN thing
E.

> marina@lagalleria.it
> Liliana is okay with it?

press@castello.it
Liliana is taking a refresher course in kick boxing . . .
let me call you, what's your direct line again?
E.

"Hmm?"

"Hmm."

"This morning I caught one of Liliana's interns trying to steal my bicycle."

"Do you think she masterminded the theft?"

"He said: 'It had fallen over, I was picking it up . . .' can you believe it?"

"Come on . . . an intern who steals bicycles to get back at someone, what on earth?"

"His internship ends today."

"What were you doing with a bicycle?"

"I go everywhere with my bicycle."

"But . . . is that a good idea? At your age? And don't you have lots of snow up there?"

"Little one, you may not remember this, but I am in in-cred-i-bly good shape for my age . . . that's why Liliana does kickboxing; to keep up with me . . ."

"Well, I think she does it to preserve her sanity. I mean, the poor woman, just imagine, there you are, constantly around, at home and at work . . ."

"Next Tuesday she's coming down to see the exhibit, you can ask her yourself."

"You're not coming?"

"We'll see."

"After work, I'm going to Procida."

"To see friends?"

"With Biagio, I'm taking the last ferry, we're leaving Agnese with her grandparents."

He simply said goodbye to her, as he had often done just before the weekend, as if the weekend were a private space he wouldn't invade, and workdays were the only time in which they could interact.

"And no matter what you say, we've only had one day of snow this year, okay?"

Marina hung up the phone and, as she closed the door to her office behind her, it seemed as if she were drawing a curtain, walking off the stage that was their shared territory, while waiting for real life to show up, all of a sudden, on Sunday afternoon.

And there had never been so many Sunday afternoons as there were in her marriage.

A whirlwind of activity: drying forks and putting them away in their drawers, chasing nephews and nieces into their bedrooms, finding the most comfortable position on the sofa. The last twenty pages of the novel, saved for the best, the quietest time, when she noticed that her parents had grown old as they toddled off for a nap. When Biagio organized the kids into teams to weed the big vases, and light settled gently onto the pages, like a cat in the winter, accompanying the words to the very last line, to the final period. The last period, where she closed her eyes and dropped off into a guiltless slumber, because she supported the world that revolved around her with her eyes, by keeping them open, but on Sunday afternoon she managed to close them with the promise that the world would manage very well on its own. That the coffee pot, filled with water and fresh coffee, sitting on the stove would wait until five thirty, and that Biagio, looking in on her as she slept from the terrace, would tell the children to play quietly.

The last ferry for Procida sailed from Pozzuoli: on the second day, with his shoulders in flames, Biagio watched it return to the island, yellow as a mail boat navigating the fjords of Norway. Marina had gone out to find a signal for her cell phone so that she could call the grandparents; as she clambered up toward the old prison she thought to herself that she didn't really like the beach so much; it was more that she loved the prickly pears that grow out of the tufa stone of Terra Murata, and the old women going in early to Sunday Mass, and the bicycles. She had rented one. She rode it back to the house, ringing the bell under the bedroom balcony.

Then Biagio lowered the thesis of Monday's doctoral candidate that he was reading and looked at her from a distance, from a vantage point much further away than the bedroom wall. He looked at her from six years of marriage, and he couldn't find her.

"I've never seen you ride a bicycle."

"In the city it's impossible . . . does it suit me?"

"Beautifully. Where'd you get it?"

"At the bike rental place. Twenty-four hours, ten euros."

"You want to get ready for dinner?"

"I'll come up."

"Then you'll give me a ride, between your arms . . ."

They had drunk plentifully and well, and then the Greco was chilled and they were still warm from the heat of the day, then the cats were begging for anchovy tails, the children were chasing after the tails of the cats around her bicyle, and then Marina got up and went into the bathroom. She locked the door and stood in front of the mirror.

She touched her face and recognized herself.

She looked into her own eyes and didn't want to leave the room. She cared less about the entire little port awaiting her outside the restaurant, about the majolica-tiled domes topping the homes that the fishermen had carved out of the earth, about Biagio dropping fish bones to the cats while smiling at the waiters, or about her own house, sleeping quietly somewhere along the coastline, Agnese sleeping in a bed with her grandmother for at least the past two hours; or again about her skin, scalding hot beneath the straps of her dress, and the freckles that had exploded with the first sunlight: she cared less about all these things than she did about the bicycle that was such a normal part of life in Turin but never in her own life. She knew that now; while she was renting it, she hadn't stopped to wonder what had prompted her whim, but now she knew: and now she started to smile.

Looking into the mirror, she covered her face with her hands, leaving just enough room between her fingers to go on looking at herself, not to lose herself, and she smiled as if she had understood and was ashamed, like someone who has done something she shouldn't but has already forgiven herself.

"Grandma told Mamma," Agnese said to her imaginary friend.

So grandmother and mother had fought, Marina understood that she had made a mistake by leaving Agnese at such a delicate juncture, allowing the child's imagination to expand and fill her grandparents' home without the embankments of her arms to contain it: grandmother had allowed Agnese to set the table for four, had let her bring a plate and a glass to the table for *Daniele*. Marina tried to explain: "The friend has to stay invisible, otherwise the child will become confused about the dimensions of reality . . . do you remember Barnaby?"

Then her phone vibrated three times in her pocket, she

gave grandmother a quick kiss, grabbed the bag with Agnese's things, and took the elevator downstairs.

the delegation is coming next week. I'm being sent to Basel. Updates in real time: call you later.

And he had called her, later. He told her he didn't know when, but he would come, alone. That he certainly would be incapable of making his way around such a complicated city alone. And Marina had sensed danger in that word: *alone.*

She could feel the danger drawing closer, silently, like water seeping into the cracks in a wall.

She'd cheated before, she knew how it was done. It hadn't been bad, but on the other hand it wasn't as spare and exquisite as her curator's sense of perfection demanded her life be, either. So strong was her belief that not a hint of those betrayals had penetrated into her life that she had never been obliged to lie, to conceal herself, to cancel memories. She had never needed to forget or omit names in the presence of others: what had happened could be contained within her body alone. Beyond that: into her home, to Biagio, to Agnese, nothing had ever filtered.

And she had told Ernesto about that betrayal, she had done it because it was a part of her life that he could not know about unless she had prompted him.

Because in the first summer that they had something to say to each other, she had let him sense her profound anguish at the idea of putting Agnese into a public daycare facility in southern Italy.

"By now she's probably already working as a courier for the Camorra . . ."

"Ha, ha, funny guy . . ."

"Does she still wear diapers?"

"Of course she doesn't. She's four years old."

"Diapers are very useful for drug traffickers . . ."

He had made her laugh, taken her mind off things, and they had finished their aperitifs arguing over an exhibit design; then she had gone back to her table, in the same piazza, fifty feet away, with the same yellow tablecloth and the same topics of conversation, sensing that her feelings of anguish over Agnese had been carefully protected by his irony, by a tenderness he had shown that constituted an unbreakable pact, a tenderness that no one else could have guessed at in Ernesto, watching him half an hour later as he refused to agree to an interview with the editor-in-chief of the most influential monthly on the market.

There was one more thing: telling him about her betrayal was a way of reminding him that there were other men in her life as well.

But it was better that Ernesto of all people should be kept there: at a safe distance, stuck behind a desk that she had never seen. Still, she could imagine it—she'd seen other desks at the Castello.

She had shifted her image of him around in her mind until it had taken on a certain substance: and now when he picked up the receiver to answer her call, he did it with *that* hand, with *that* light coming from the left. As for what she really thought, she had no real idea: all of the sensors and receptors that allowed her to glimpse an affair between colleagues long before those involved had noticed a thing, the dolorous antennae that had allowed her to predict her sister-in-law's divorce months before the rest of the family, that helped her to foresee Biagio's problems and malaises, were now overloaded, occluded, good for nothing.

She'd have to ask someone else, the way she did with her colleagues when she had spent too much time on a reproduction and could no longer say whether or not it was worth buying, when she needed help understanding how much she really liked the things she liked. That's what she needed to do: ask what those signals, those phone calls meant, ask for an interpretation, and—like a fortune teller peering into the bottom of a teacup—hope for a clear response.

She tried not calling him. For days she answered his messages as tersely as possible, just enough to keep him from understanding that something was wrong.

It had happened before, and it never lasted long.

A cycle of resistance that never extended more than a week. For Marina it was like when you stop smoking after a bad spell of coughing: she could bury the thought of it under the blanket of passing days until she had convinced herself that she was fine, that she was better.

But as soon as she was fine, as soon as she was better, then she no longer had a good reason not to call him.

press@castello.it
Well, they're on their way. Liliana's with them.
You think you'll go to the museum?
Or are you going to send that genius Donati?
Liliana planned everything out like a school field trip: they'll walk around the museum, take a couple of polaroids, then at noon someone'll say: "now, where can we go for a nice pizza?" No one will notice if you don't show up . . . I'm coming down next Wednesday.
E.

Marina rescheduled the inspection at the museum, moving it up two hours, so that she could check the progress of the decomposition of the cow's head. The museum attendants were complaining about the stench and a Danish tourist had fainted when she saw the swarming maggots.

She rescheduled her lunch date, by the time she came level with the Cinema Adriano she'd given up hope that the taxi would make any more progress in traffic, and she walked uphill, all the way to the end of Via Sant'Anna dei Lombardi.

The stone piazza was exploding in the bright sunlight, old men were trying to play a game of *tresette*, matching cards in the shade of the sole banana tree to survive the aesthetic slaughter of a Milanese architect.

The attendants greeted Marina's arrival as if they had been standing around by a clogged cesspool, waiting for a septic pump truck; she calmed them with one raised hand as she stepped through the turnstile at the entrance, and walked into Hall II just as the Dottoressa Donati began presenting the *problem* to the delegation from the Castello.

Marina walked toward them with the confidence of the owner of the house, smiling and taking for granted that her name, announced once by La Donati, amply served in place of all the handshakes, and looking only at Liliana, explained why the artist had chosen *not* to have the blood drained.

At noon, someone said: "Now, where can we go for a nice pizza?"

Later, Marina accompanied them to the other exhibition.

The other show had no stench, but none of the guests would have dared to leave town without being able to say they had seen it. They managed to work up some interest, even though there hadn't been a market in Caravaggio's since 1610.

As soon as Marina could, she looked out into the park: she'd forgotten what it was to hate a woman, to fear her.

She remembered furious jealousies from her adolescence that had eventually been reconciled into a feeling of sisterhood, the confidence of a shared vocabulary, an affiliation that no one needed to betray or fear; indeed, a protective relationship.

And men, too: they had been transmogrified into a homogeneous and monolithic world of shared characteristics.

They talked to one another through their women. Sons-in-law and fathers-in-law, brothers and brothers-in-law, husbands whose wives were friends, husbands—once friends with other husbands—now decided what to do on Saturdays and summer vacations through their women. Which Christmas presents, what movie theater, the bottle of wine to bring for the dinner party. They recognized one another from the attitudes and stances that the women recognized in them, they ribbed one another with the nicknames that their own women had assigned them.

And, having become these people, even the men were no longer fearsome.

It had been years, a great many long years, since there had been a human being who inspired fear in her.

That fear that now moved elegantly in a calf-length skirt, smiling beneath the sort of brick-red lipstick that only stops being crass once you've turned forty. When it suddenly becomes a mark of a respectable, intellectual bourgeoisie. A woman who knows how to wear lipstick of this sort has permanently relegated any other female being that may enter her sphere to a subaltern status. And in fact, that was how Marina felt now: an apprentice girl who would never attain the full mastery of her years and her beauty.

This woman, Liliana, had something extra, and perhaps what set her apart more than anything else was the fact that she had resisted the temptation to have children. Perhaps it had never occurred to her to plan on them, and she had never given in to the loss of her own identity. The fact that Ernesto had never sensed that impulse in Liliana made her special, stronger.

And what was especially humiliating to Marina, sitting at an angle to the window and looking out over the pine trees, was not only Liliana and the twelve years she had been living with Ernesto, slapped down right in front of her, there, by the Medusa's head, but the larger universe that she couldn't see, about which she received reports days afterward.

Marina looked out over the pines that plunged down toward the city from the parapet of the Belvedere. And she felt an obscure longing for herself.

The present moment never seemed to arrive for her: it was the pressure that the nape of the neck lacks an instant before a caress, the empty phone line waiting for that special call to come so that it could buzz "busy," the gap in sleep upon awakening the morning of the excursion.

When Ernesto was due to arrive in just three days, calm suddenly prevailed.

Marina regained mastery over her distance from things, and made preparations for the coming encounter, just as she had for the last inauguration.

She made reservations at one restaurant for dinner, at another for lunch.

She alerted the grandparents for Wednesday afternoon, she'd drop off Agnese at three, with everything that she'd need until the next day: "Mamma, Biagio is at a conference."

"But weren't you supposed to coordinate your travel schedules, you and your husband?"

She imagined where they would go, where they'd begin, when they'd begin. She asked La Donati: "Is the Montesanto funicular railway running again?" She kept her voice neutral, emotionless as she asked.

She walked through her house, looking around her, imagining it as an unfamiliar place, so she could figure out what didn't work, the way she did when she entered and left finished museum halls, workers seated on the ground, the artist outside catching a smoke.

She purchased a square tobacco-scented bar of soap and began using it, to keep it from looking brand new, so that when Biagio came home from his conference he wouldn't wonder what had happened to the liquid soap.

She moved the kitchen chair against the wall, because she was planning to make a cup of coffee for him.

She checked in her dresser drawer to make sure that she had the right bra to be glimpsed through the blouse, and dropped the pair of panties that went with the bra into the washing machine, because, while he might never know, she would.

Then she called the cleaning woman and asked her to

come in that Monday as well, and to wax all the floors; then she played a game with Agnese, a game they only played in the winter: dragging felt pads underfoot all over the house, as if they were skating over the newly waxed tiles.

On Wednesday morning, Marina bought red gerber daisies because they stood out nicely against the ocher-colored wall. Once she had made the whole house neat and orderly, she began to invent a subtle disarray, because that disarray was her way of revealing herself. Her way of telling him that she had listened to a new jazz version of Bach, that she had fertilized her geranium plants for the summer, and researched a recipe for cod just the night before, in the Carnacina & Veronelli cookbook lying open on the kitchen table, that she had left her nightgown in the bathroom, hanging by its straps from the door handle.

Then she shampooed her hair and went to pick up Agnese at school.

"Agnese get your book bag: your mother is here . . . Signora, today she really went too far."

"What do you mean?"

"We set an extra plate for her . . ."

"She's gotten used to that; it's true, her grandparents have spoiled her."

"Yes, but today she wanted her teacher to put food on the plate."

"She's never asked for that before—"

"She wouldn't eat until we filled up *Daniele*'s plate too. Signora, you realize how absurd this is?"

"Of course I understand, and you're right—"

"Then it really creeped me out . . . that plate, sitting

there, with no one seated in front of it . . . it had an odd effect on the other children too."

"No, you are certainly right, I need to have a talk with her."

"You certainly have resources: your husband is a doctor."

"This isn't pathological. It's just that she has a vivid imagination."

"And there's nothing wrong with imagination, but we can't indulge it past a certain point . . . See what you can work out."

Afterwards, as she hurried along the sidewalk, guarding the child against traffic with her body even as she marched along briskly, tugging her by the hand, Marina sensed that this was not the right time to kindle any conflict with either Agnese or Biagio. She would make passing reference to it with the grandparents, at the front door, without saying anything the child might understand. If only Ernesto hadn't called her at that very moment, if only she hadn't asked him:

"Where are you?"

"In Turin."

"When's your flight?"

"There's no way I can come."

"You can't—why? . . . No, I mean, really."

"You're right, I know."

"Are you okay?"

"Yes, it's just that they stuck me with Paul Smith at the last minute, no one else can squire him around . . . and to think that I don't even like his shirts."

"I'm so sorry."

"Oh well, there are other shirts."

" . . . "

"I'm sorry, too . . . shall we try again next week?"

" . . . "

"You still there?"

"Here's what let's try. Let's try: you never call me again."

"You mean that?"

"I mean that."

"I don't know if I can manage that."

"I'm sure you can."

Admitting it.

Admitting it without slowing her stride—that was hard to do: but the instant she knew he wasn't coming, she remembered that she had piled up her hours, working an exhausting shift so that she could be free for him, that she had clipped the hanging lamp wire, two days before the new fixture would be delivered, lest he see it that way, and that she had stood looking at the chili pepper bush, thinking how pretty it would be if, among all the green peppers, there were only one red chili.

That she had read the forecasts in *La Repubblica* weather page, seeking among the uncertainties of the little *day after tomorrow* clouds the certainty of nice weather—not so he would think she was always surrounded by nice weather, but because on every sunny day, Marina had thought of him.

"Mamma's crying," Agnese told her imaginary friend.

2.

The painter called her for the third time in ten minutes, and she summoned the interpreter. For the third time in ten minutes, the painter had applied three different shades of white paint on a white wall. Marina made a special effort, looked intently, tipping her head to look with the light and against the light, but she still couldn't see any difference. It was white. She selected the one in the middle: "*Richtig,*" she said, without help from the interpreter, and then smiled a smile that registered approval of the effort, rather than the result.

That was all the painter wanted: he retied the strings on his white smock and climbed back up onto the scaffolding to apply the final coat. Marina kept thinking that at this rate they'd never be done; she felt a pressure in her chest and stepped outside for a cigarette. The air in the hall was so redolent of solvents that if she lit the cigarette inside, they'd all be blown sky high. Her, the artists, and the painter who was dressed with an elegance that not even doctors dreamed of, back in Naples.

She stood thinking about that explosion, and it made her feel better, she watched as bits and pieces of herself lofted into the air; her head wobbled slightly as she traced their trajectories: the pieces of her executed perfect parabolic curves and tumbled down onto the trees in the garden, into the little lake, into the terracotta tiled courtyard of the former brewery. Every time that one of the pieces reached the apex of its trajectory, Marina looked up, blew out a stream of cigarette smoke, and glanced at the tip of the TV tower in the Alexanderplatz. The last piece fell beyond the wall; Marina imagined a dog, his paws sticky with asphalt, seizing the last piece in its jaws and trotting off with it, then she put out her cigarette and waded back into the fray, to resume the battle with colors and languages.

She dragged herself to dinner, wearing the same jeans, the same pockets filled with packing straw, with her measured weariness. Her riveted concentration, maintained unwavering for hours, her ability to hold suspended in her mind the next step of the process for as long as it took to complete the current step; that too, had its measure. At the end of the day, the weariness of management had a different savor, she allowed herself the satisfaction. It wasn't like the blind exhaustion with which manual laborers finished their day, going home without even being able to sit down for a minute on the crates, because the spine no longer remembers what it is to rest.

But sitting at the dinner table, as her anxiety subsided, Marina detected a blip, a misunderstanding: she was no longer interested in what she was doing.

Since June, work no longer interested her, eating no longer interested her if she couldn't tell Ernesto about all the different dishes, about the waiter's uniform, about the sculptor hunched over his plate as if he were in the dining hall of a rest home. Marina lived her days and had to take them for what they were, she could hardly spend time thinking about them, or making a special effort to remember, setting them aside for tomorrow, archiving them to report on them later. Everything had to be sufficient unto the day: like a lake restrained by a dam. That was how Marina had worked to tamp down those months of absence, restoring everything to normal, controllable, clearly defined dimensions.

She dined lightly; she was beginning to feel a hunger for vegetables and olive oil, she was beginning to feel like cooking again. She went back to the hotel and called Biagio, talked for a long time to Agnese, and then fell asleep.

Once again, she got no rest that night: she fell asleep right away, but a few hours later she was wide awake, her right hand throbbing dully, and she lay there in bed, too weak to read or sit up; she left the light off, lay in the dark. She felt it was necessary, inevitable to go home, the girl falling asleep between them, Biagio consoling her: "It's carpal tunnel syndrome, women are especially prone to it," she said it to herself over and over, as she clenched and relaxed her fist in the dark, as she tried turning onto her other side, using her other hand to bring feeling back into her fingers.

Women are prone to it, but in a hotel room bed, that explanation was no longer convincing. That hand just got too tired; but the installation would be finished soon: from there to the last few polaroids, to the first digital shots that she'd download and send to Biagio, and from then to the moment when the ambassador walked into the hall, when she would have to ask room service to give her suit a quick pressing, would be just a few days.

On the plane, knowing she was on her way home, she would sleep at least as far as Malpensa airport, outside Milan.

She fell asleep again and dreamed the last fairytale she had read to Agnese before leaving, when her daughter had sensed that the next day they would be saying goodbye again, and had asked for a story, then for her hand, and she had been afraid to fall asleep, to let her mother go, her mother who—she knew—would be leaving for Berlin before she woke up. Before she had her milk, and saw her grandmother, and went to nursery school, Mamma would already be at the airport.

"Mamma's leaving tomorrow," she had explained to her imaginary friend. "But she'll be back."

And then, finally, she'd fallen asleep. That evening Marina had read Agnese the story of a little Flemish boy who had saved his village, in a valley below a lake, by plugging up with his child's finger a leak in the dike that dammed the waters. It was a sad story, a story that demanded excessive heroism. It was a fairytale that Agnese's grandmother had given her. Marina had sharply criticized her mother's choice of that book, she had condemned it as "nineteenth century," meaning that there was no remedy for the gap of times and intentions that had opened between the two of them. But after a while the book had proven to be quite useful, it had a singsong cadence, and the phrases ended with vague assonances, not particularly attractive, but they helped the girl get to sleep.

And now Marina was dreaming it: she was her own voice reading somewhere and at the same time she was a woman trying to plug the leak with her hand, protecting her village down in the valley, the girl waiting for her to come back. She was plugging the hole, exhausting work though it was, and the water flowed out between her fingers in rivulets and streams, and so she jammed her hand even harder against the dike, until she finally dropped off, losing consciousness.

"As soon as I get back, I'm going to have my hand X-rayed," she said aloud, to wake herself up and so that it was an order to herself, then she went to smear some Orudis gel on her wrist, along the tunnel that was pinching her nerves, the way Biagio had taught her to do.

He finally called her. He did it in the evening.

It was her last night there, and Marina had found only one shoe in her suitcase, she'd rummaged and searched, then she called Biagio and asked him to look for her black patent-leather flats: she could only find one shoe of the pair. The other one was still at home. Biagio was holding it in his hand when he called her back. There wasn't even time to laugh at the situation; she shot out the door, caught a taxi to a shopping mall, the only place that was still open in Berlin at 7:40 in the evening. There she was: an Italian, trying on shoes you might expect to find in a supermarket, without half sizes.

She arrived at the inauguration late and breathless, but decently attired. She had to smile a little more often, spend more time with people she'd never have given the time of day—to make up for the shoes.

She closed ranks and maintained parade ground discipline as long as necessary. Certainly, this was a social event, but behind it lay three weeks of work, shoulder to shoulder with the construction workers, and that had to be clear to everyone. She maintained a scholarly tone with the directors of other museums, a ceremonial tone with the institutional officials, and she represented the Gallery with every word she spoke. At the same time, unfailingly, she represented herself as well. She never said "we" to indicate the staff for whom she worked, but every time that she said "I" it was clear that she was referring to an array of forces behind her to whom she was grateful. She *wasn't* the

Gallery, but she was the only person the Gallery had chosen to represent it.

Nor did she forget that this inauguration was the artist's party, and she left center stage for him. She watched him from afar, toasting with the other dealers, like the wife of a very handsome man, happy to let other women flirt with him, as long as she feels certain that she alone will be warming his bed.

The wine seemed to hit everybody at the same instant, and that was the sign that the tension was finally broken, the games over, the alliances formed, and that everything that was absolutely essential had happened.

Then Marina allowed people to notice her shoulders and her neck, allowed them to pour her a glass of Sicilian red imported for the occasion, let an architect offer to walk her out onto the terrace for a smoke.

"I'll get my shawl."

And emerging from the thirteenth floor of a building overlooking the lights of Berlin, Marina thought that it hardly seemed like October.

She brought her hands to her cheeks as if to take their temperature, and she calculated to the tenth of a percent the degree of coquetterie and cunning she brought to the mix—*the perfect amount to share the view with someone, not enough to share a bed*—as she asked: "Are my cheeks red?"

At that moment, Ernesto called her.
"Hello?"
"Is this a bad time?"
"Is that you?"
"Disappointed?"

"But . . . why are you calling from an 02 number?"

"I'm in Milan until Monday."

"How are you?"

"Oh . . . well . . . I miss you."

"Duly noted."

"Okay, but I did manage to find a good excuse to call you."

"Which is?"

"I received the press release for the inauguration."

"Ah, congratulations . . . and so?"

"I wanted to tell you to break a leg."

"That leg snapped neatly in half four hours ago, but thanks all the same."

"Isn't the opening tomorrow?"

"Darling, tomorrow is when the show opens to the *public*. And while people are standing in line outside this building, I'll be on the plane, out cold . . . I plan to sleep straight through to Malpensa Airport."

"Did it wear you out?"

"That's not it, I've been sleeping badly, I wake up in the middle of the night with no feeling in my right hand."

"It must be carpal tunnel syndrome: women are prone to it."

"Did you have a girlfriend who was an orthopedist?"

"I've had lots of girlfriends with carpal tunnel syndrome. What time do you land at Malpensa?"

"Couldn't say."

"I'll come out to the airport."

"Don't be ridiculous: I have a connecting flight for Naples."

"Half an hour?"

"Don't be a dope."

"Send me a message when you know what time you're getting in."

"I won't be leaving the transit area."

"I'll bribe the guy who watches the gate."

"But tomorrow's Sunday . . . aren't there soccer matches?"

"Hadn't thought of that, silly me: Inter is playing in Turin today—a home game."

To realize that she hadn't brought anything suitable. Nothing that had the appearance that she wanted to project: the sort of woman who flies in comfortable but elegant clothing, who sleeps soundly while the attendants bring pastries down the aisle, who only selects foreign newspapers from the pile offered by the attendants.

Where was the right dress to see him again, spend two hours with him? What overcoat would be appropriate to welcome his embrace? Marina thought it over until dawn, mentally reviewing the floor plan of Tegel airport, straining to remember in which terminal she had seen Gucci, and then she assembled everything she had in her suitcases, the skirt with the blouse, but also the same blouse with the pair of pants. Like with the paper dress-up dolls when she was little, she carefully cut out from the closet background all her clothing and tried them on all night long, and she did it to take her mind off it, to muddle her thoughts, to keep from thinking that in just ten hours, the automatic doors of the arrivals terminal would whoosh open into Sunday afternoon.

As she was walking along the moving walkway, she thought to herself: he won't come. But even if he didn't, it wouldn't change a thing. Marina was telling herself that now nothing could change, and that the food court in the departure terminal would in any case be better than the hot dog she'd be forced to settle for in the transit area.

She tried to gauge the normality of her actions by the people who watched her walk past telephone booths and restrooms, who watched her step into the aisle marked "nothing to declare": nobody else noticed anything strange.

Only Marina noticed that the automatic doors seemed to yawn open disastrously rather than slide open, as if the water had finally vanquished the dike and, in a thunderous roar of teetering foam, was rushing down into the valley below.

She moved toward him like a blank sheet of paper, with the expression that she used to wear at university on exam days, as she walked into the hall and focused on a sheet of white paper to keep from focusing on anything else. Like actors when they tire themselves out before the curtain, to keep from feeling the fear.

"Ciao."

"Ciao."

"Hungry?"

"Not really: they stuffed us on the plane."

"How about an espresso?"

Then they walked by a newsstand, and decided to step inside to leaf through a few interior decoration magazines; he edged over a little closer, to take a look at the same majolica stove on the same page, and he draped a hand over her hip. She placed her hand firmly over his, holding the hand in place where he had chosen to lay it, for a long time. And they both stood there gazing at the stove. She finally closed the magazine when he kissed her.

Malpensa Airport on a Sunday afternoon seemed like a hospital, the terminals filled with sick passengers waiting to leave.

Ernesto ate a grilled cheese sandwich while Marina sipped an espresso because, though she was hungry, she knew she couldn't swallow a bite, and didn't want him to notice. She managed to clasp his hand in hers on the table, but even as she did, she sensed her happiness was less than complete. She could feel a fever raging inside her, and the fever was him but also his absence: they had a windfall of two hours to spend together, time that she had been craving for months, until she no longer even wanted it, and yet she couldn't rid herself of the knowledge that it would only be two hours.

Even love, now that it had returned, had become adult. It was learning to discipline itself, when necessary, but in exchange when it arrived it no longer exploded. It was no longer an isolated, blinding flash of light: it brought everything else with it.

The anguish filled the flat, lowering sky to which neither of them was accustomed; it lurked among the few, scattered cars in the endless checkerboard of the parking area. Airplanes taking off, airplanes landing, windsocks.

Marina allowed him to kiss her neck, in the fear and hope that he would soon stop, she let him run his thumb along her neckline, she let it graze the nipple of one breast. She longed and yearned to hold it there, but she was only happy when she was walking once again toward the departure gate, when he walked her to the escalator and she knew that he was behind her, watching her rise up the moving staircase, and—confident in the knowledge—she did not turn to look behind her.

As she fastened her seatbelt, her mind was still empty. Not a thought to the fact that she was departing, not a thought to where she was going next. Not a thought of what they had said to one another, of how they had said goodbye, of their appointment to meet again in Bologna, nor did she think about the fact that her husband was in the car right now, as the airplane rose into the air, to make sure that he made it around the Naples Bypass while the crowds were still leaving the soccer stadium, in order to be at the airport in time to meet her.

She fell asleep while the flight attendants were serving chocolates.

She was on the bypass with Biagio, and together they looked with relief at the cars clogging the opposite lanes; beneath them, the remaining light followed the city down to the sea. Marina rested her left hand on her husband's thigh.

"Are you tired?"

"Mmm, exhausted . . . but everything went well."

"Did you wear your slippers to the inauguration?"

"The ugliest pair of shoes I ever bought . . ."

But the greatest pleasure of coming home was taking Agnese in her arms: she carried the child with her to the king-sized bed, opened the suitcase as Agnese watched, and let her burrow and rummage among the stockings and sweaters to find the gifts she had brought for her.

"I brought you a comic book; Grandpa brought it back for me from one of his trips, when I was little."

Barnaby had colors designed to captivate children of another era, but Agnese took it in both hands as if she had sensed that there were more things inside than the cover promised. And she smiled.

"I'll read it to you tomorrow."

"I can read it to myself."

"It's in English, Mamma will read it to you, and then you'll learn to read it on your own."

The apartment looked wonderful, she decided it had done nicely even without her, and late that night, when Biagio pulled her down onto the sofa, Marina was more potent than when she had left.

She could feel the power between her legs as she wrapped them around his hips, she sensed that she could afford to allow it to happen on the sofa. On any other ordinary conjugal evening, they would have been obliged to respect the rituals: the bed, and closing the door, and her going briefly into the bathroom beforehand, but now something that had kept them at a distance had snapped, and it was Marina.

She felt a childish excitement sweep over her, and as they made love she dragged everything that surrounded her into her happiness. She swept her husband into that happiness and emptied her mind of everything: all she wanted was to keep on feeling that happiness.

The words they had said at the airport, the desire unearthed from the core of her body, poured out.

For two hours, at Malpensa Airport, life had been what she'd imagined, and this power—nothing else—was what Marina was projecting around herself, onto the apartment walls, onto Agnese, even onto Biagio.

Only later, in the final embrace, did Ernesto surface

from the murky depths of that joy, and Marina looked at him, arraying his features over her husband's face, and taking great care to say nothing, because the only thing she could have said was his name.

An hour later, Biagio was massaging her wrist with Orudis gel.

"' . . . But evidently they didn't believe I was up to the standards of the Gallery's reputation . . .'—can you believe that asshole?"

La Donati's voice was trembling as if she really cared.

"Well, okay, but it's true: we never liked his work . . ."

"But did he need to say that in a newspaper interview?"

"Exactly: so now he's the one who looks like a jerk."

"Excuse me, can I read the rest? He even tells them the numbers . . ."

"No, look, it all strikes me as extremely distasteful . . ."

"Listen, listen to this: 'the worst behind-the-scenes aspect of the negotiations is the economic risk . . .'"

Marina understood that the best way to free herself from the ordeal was to let her read, and as she listened, she let her mind drift back, remembering Ernesto's thumb on her nipple.

In those brief seconds in which his thumb had grazed the nipple, he had changed it: now she felt it firm and full beneath her T-shirt, she knew that it was still beautiful, even though she had forgotten to do the collagen applications that Biagio's colleague had suggested after nursing Agnese. She smiled.

"Sure, you go ahead and laugh . . . it doesn't matter to you because you were in Berlin, but I can't tell you the phone calls I've had to listen to . . ."

*

She did some rapid calculations: attending the Bologna workshop would be a natural opportunity to see him again.

By then, her period would have just ended: it would start on Wednesday, Thursday at the very latest, with a morning rush to the bathroom, and four days later there'd be nothing but blood-tinged mucus, acceptable to anyone, even the first time they would be together. Ever since she had given birth to Agnese, her periods had been regular, much lighter, no longer the devastating inundation that swept her into bed for three days of every month. After the pregnancy, her body had become less extreme.

"So when are you getting in?"

"The morning of the fifteenth, I think: I have a few appointments with . . . what about you?"

"I'm taking the train on the nineteenth."

"Why so late?"

"The workshop starts on the twentieth."

"But I'm getting there on the fifteenth."

"You said that already . . . so?"

"You're so pretty when you get mad . . ."

"Pretty? I wouldn't say that, I'm bloated, my eyes are all puffy . . ."

She took a bath, because the weather was turning cold, making a lot of things possible: to stop taking showers, to wear stockings under her skirt again, to serve slightly thicker soups at dinner, in an attempt to convince Agnese to eat vegetables.

She filled the tub and plunged into it, soaking for a long

time, her nose flush with the surface of the warm water, surrounded on all sides by the distant noises of the neighbors moving their tables for dinner.

She stood up, emerging from the water to inspect her legs: even in terms of hair-length, the timing for Bologna was ideal.

She loved being back home more than ever. Now time gave itself to her in another manner; everything she did was a series of little votive gifts for Ernesto.

She shattered the hard crust of sea salt in which she had baked the fish as if he were right there, watching her from behind a kitchen tile. She picked up her wineglass as if he had just filled it for her, tasted the wine as if Ernesto were her lips, her tongue, her very taste.

In those first days of school, Marina stayed home in the afternoons to welcome Agnese home, to assuage her new anxieties: the child came home every day, worried by the new wave of demands and challenges, eager to do well, exhausted from the intense concentration. She was so frustrated by her inability to link her "g" and her "o" the way the teacher had shown the class on the blackboard that when she came home on Friday, she simply collapsed on the floor, just inside the front door. And so Marina picked her up and persuaded her that it wasn't so important to connect the two curving lines after all. She'd written in Agnese's notebook: "you're a good good girl all the same," to show her that it was true in her writing as well as out.

Only after that was Agnese willing to eat her dinner. Then she explained to *Daniele* the right way to do the homework.

So the household felt a new peacefulness, even though

the new energy that had brought that peace was also push-
ing the family straight toward an abyss: family relations
tend to skirt questions about their own inner workings, as
long as they function smoothly.

Then she felt it. She was sitting in an easy chair one
afternoon, watching Agnese read: she was still moving her
lips to shape the words, but she was already controlling
her voice, and Marina allowed herself to be hypnotized by
those succinct movements, by the child's body rocking
gently back and forth from the waist.

It was only because of this that it happened, that she
began to perk her ears up to catch a far-away signal, like
those times on the drive to Amalfi, just before the last
curve around the mountain pass, when there was something imperceptible in the air, when she could sense the
sea even before she first glimpsed it.

Marina felt her second child.

She knew with such certainty that the tiny twinge she
felt was not the onset of her period that, two days later, she
watched calmly and without doubt as the test tube tinged
with color, as slowly as the cigarette that smoldered in her
other hand.

She stood up from her perch on the rim of the bathtub,
and thought back to Biagio on the sofa, his features dis-
solving and forming the face of Ernesto, Ernesto who
would be boarding a train for Bologna just two hours from
now, who in three days would be waiting for her outside
her hotel: he would open the door of her taxi cab, embrace
her in the lobby, take the suitcase from her hand, and
speak the few words necessary in the time it took to check
in at the reception desk. Then he would again embrace

her, this time definitively, in the elevator going up, and from then on.

She stood there, looking out the window at a city where there was no longer a single street you could stroll along: it was pointless to go out, and anyway it was starting to rain, and people got frantic when it rained, crowding lobbies and doorways at the first drop, as if they were made of spun sugar. She continued staring out the window until her legs began to ache, and she was happy to be able to sit down, to have a reason to return to the easy chair.

She didn't know how to tell Biagio. She was pregnant with a legitimate child, from her legitimate husband, at a reasonable age. She didn't know how to explain that she had embraced another man, that her child would not be able to recognize its father, because she herself couldn't recognize Biagio as the father.

But what was tormenting Marina most was not the absurdity of trying to persuade Biagio that a child conceived with him was not really his child. The problem was explaining to Ernesto that it really was his.

All of that pain turned into the impossibility of bearing a child to a man with whom she had never gone to bed. The fact that, even though she had thought always and only of him, and had never renounced him, never abandoned his love, that child was not his.

Marina wrapped herself in the warm coverlet and wept bitterly for her new child, an infant in the space of three short weeks had had to accept within itself her own life, and the lives of Ernesto, Biagio, and Agnese.

She wept the way she wept sometimes for the children who beg at the corner of the Piazza Borsa, or who play the hurdy-gurdy in the subway, obliged to display the wrongs of one and all with their single bodies. And she wept for her child because she could not hate it.

The world was full of women who'd done it for worse or better reasons than hers, and she was a part of that world. But that was the last thing she said to herself as she boarded the plane, because when Marina was being overwhelmed by tension and stress, instead of snapping, she became distracted. And so she landed in Cologne when the lights of the shops were flickering on, and she thought that this would be the perfect time of year to visit the Christmas Market. To buy candles and wooden stars and the trolls that Agnese liked so much. The right latitude at the right time of year, and so Marina forgot why she had come and called Biagio stretched out on the bed in the room as if she were in a hotel room, and complained that the art dealer would be two days late, as if it were the truth.

She called Agnese's grandmother, too, because it was almost Christmas and they hadn't made any plans at all. They hadn't planned at whose houses they'd be spending Christmas Eve, Christmas Day, and St. Stephen's; nor had they decided who would buy the fish for the Christmas dinner, or who would buy candy and pastries. She ended the call with a piece of advice: "Mamma, Agnese already has too many Barbies."

All that needed to be removed was a translucent sphere no bigger than the tip of a ballpoint pen.

The surgeon placed it on a glass slide. Then he left the anesthesiologists to bring Marina back to consciousness, and went back to his office.

He took off his white coat, washed his hands, and sat down at his desk. Outside the window, the oak trees were scattering red leaves like so many drops of blood, because this year it had turned cold suddenly. The doctor sat looking at the leaves for a moment, then pushed the slide into the microscope and placed his right eye over the eyepiece. Enveloped in a light-blue membrane, he saw, fully outlined, the shape of a baby.

F.G.R.

Evening

Then, one day, the black-market came to an end. Since then, it's been so much more painful to go back home to my mother's. It's been like walking back along streets without landmarks. Without the bonfires in the oil drums, without the women sitting on fruit crates selling controband cigarettes, walking up Via Dante has become dark and oppressive. The cluster of young men in sleeveless shirts loitering at the corner of the alleyway selling drugs was just never the same thing—plus there isn't much activity at the time of evening that I go by. I step down from the 111 bus, at seven o'clock at the latest; the occasional junkie from one of the outlying towns who still has to make it home gets off the bus with me and walks me part of the way. I've seen them guzzle ampules of Delorazepam, sitting way in the back of the bus to ward off the fear when the 111 is inching forward in a traffic jam. We walk along together all the way to the intersection, then I continue along Corso Italia, and they stop at their supplier. I speed up because the shops are closing up for the night, and there's no good reason to be in the street after that. Until tomorrow, the street no longer exists.

When I come even with the covered market, I necessarily look ahead of me, toward the end of the street, and up: my mother. She is waiting behind the window, curtains pulled back like a theater. Her hands are on the radiator. *You're late, I was starting to worry.* I lower my eyes to the street without waving. What would it take to raise an arm, while I'm looking up at her? *Mamma, I'm still alive, and so are you.* But I can't stand her backlit silhouette. Her silhouette tells me that I'm late, that she was starting to worry, that the worry triggered one of her headaches, and now if she wants to get rid of the headache, the only way is for her to go to sleep.

At last, I cross the street: the line of balconies hides me from her gaze and protects me from the pelting rain of guilt. I ought to panhandle drops of Delorazepam from the out-of-town junkies every time I come here.

I still have the keys, ten years later. But my mother always buzzes the front door open from upstairs at the exact instant I am fitting the key into the lock.

As the elevator climbs from the fourth floor to the fifth, I rehearse what I'm going to say as soon as I see her: I have to say some ordinary thing, to try to make seeing one another again seem normal. I come up with something to cover up the awkwardness of being mother and daughter, of having emerged one out of the body of the other and then separating. Something that can wipe away the astonishment of seeing one another again, twice a week, just a few days apart. After nearly forty years, this always amazes me, it shocks my inmost being as if I were only now being born, as if we stopped living the instant we left one another's sight.

I am being born, right now, ferried into existence by this elevator. Seventh floor. I'm here. Mamma opens the door and welcomes me in.

"Hey, Mamma."

"I was starting to worry."

"Listen, on my way up I noticed that they're working on the place across from Enzo's old stall. Is that going to be his store?"

"Sure, that's him, he got a lease on it, and now he's renovating the interior."

"When I went by to get that CD for Luca, he told me he had decided to open a shop."

" . . . All that time I was waiting for you, a headache started up, the only thing I feel like doing right now is going to take a nap, oy."

As we're talking, I set down the bags and my purse, I step into the little bedroom to lay my knapsack on the bed.

"Don't make noise: Luca's in there."

I'm careful not to make noise. To look at him, Luca seems like a quiet child.

Taking care not to make noise, I move through the dark, in a room I know by heart.

It was in this very same room, right where Luca is sleeping right now, that I first convinced myself that things could only exist as long as I saw them: I was eleven years old, and I had viral hepatitis. My transaminase levels were at 800. Our family doctor from the health service said it might be a good idea to get me to a hospital. My mother said that maybe the doctor had fallen and hit his head on the pavement, maybe he should get to a hospital himself, that I would get all the care I needed at home. I spent nine days in a row in bed, but it hardly felt like a deprivation— I was exhausted the whole time. I would get up six or seven times a day, hobbling slowly, my sister Sara at my side, to go pee. My pee looked like the rust in a decrepit toilet. This was before I got my first period, and I had never seen the water tinged a dark color; it upset me.

Life went on in my home at its usual pace: from time to time, someone would step into my bedroom to ask if I wanted anything, or to bring me something, and then they'd go away. I could hear their footsteps fading into the distance, or their voice would continue speaking to me, but I began to believe that, once they crossed the threshold of my sight, people and things dissolved, ceasing the existence they had when I could still see them.

Then my pee lightened, the bilirubin levels in my blood declined, and there seemed to be no damage to my nervous system. I was left with the belief that things existed spasmodically, and a feeling of exhaustion.

"Mamma, do you remember when I got hepatitis?"

"It was when you ate mussels down by the botanical gardens."

"What were you thinking, letting an eleven-year-old girl eat mussels?"

"Why, if you were eighteen, you wouldn't have caught hepatitis?"

"But what is that supposed to mean, Mamma?"

"And we all had hepatitis markers. Even your father had them."

"Anyway, Mamma, you have a headache because this kid is trouble."

My mother went back to her post by the window, she stood like a stork on one slipper, scratching the other foot against the radiator. She's waiting for Sara. Mamma is always waiting for someone who makes her worry. I walk over to her, and I wait with her. She makes some room for me next to the radiator. We stand there, side by side, and the window guides our gazes outside, into the street, to Enzo's new shop.

"It's going to be a cell phone store."

"This I don't understand: he was in the record business, so why doesn't he set up a music store?"

"Mamma, he wasn't *in the record business*: he sold counterfeit CDs . . ."

"All right, that's true, but it's still better than when he sold contraband cigarettes."

"Okay, but it's still a crime in Italy. Now that he's setting up a store, it's going to be the first honest thing he's done in his life."

"But he's been successful."

"Those Marlboros he sold tasted like sawdust."

"When you were twelve years old, you were already smoking, and you lecture me about the mussels . . ."

"I was sixteen, Mamma. Sixteen."

I was already smoking at twelve; they had already condemned the last of the farmland, purchased the last truck gardens, flattened the citrus groves, and begun to pour the first slabs of cement, and work had begun on the construction of what we now call "the third world." The outskirts of town were inventing their own outskirts, with less and less infrastructure, where the old people could be isolated and the young could be warehoused. We would duck under the railings surrounding the construction yard, beneath the sign reading "no help wanted," and we would climb up onto the foundations of the "third world." We'd light one cigarette at a time, one for each of us girls. And then we'd watch the afternoon go by.

It was a time when smoking a cigarette on the sly still had a connotation of privacy. And another, external connotation: when you were twelve years old and a girl, going home with the smell of tobacco on your breath and your clothing meant catching a beating from your father. If you were like me, and your father had been dead for a few months, it meant your mother would flail at herself, slapping herself in the face out of shame.

"There she is."

She already said it three motorbikes ago, but this time it really is her. She comes barreling along at high speed from the intersection as if she were fifteen years old and had nothing to lose. She skids to a halt three doors up from here, right outside the ramp of the parking garage. Then she steps off the motorbike like a princess descending from her carriage on the day of the ball. Sara doesn't even need to take the motorbike down the ramp: as soon as she comes within range, she jams her thumb down furiously on the horn, even at night, and the parking attendants—far from losing their tempers—climb up the ramp with a broad smile as if she had cast a spell on them. They watch her take off her helmet as if it were a cunning little cloche with a black lace veil, and then gaze raptly as she runs her fingers through her blonde hair, in her blonde way. Then they catch the keys she tosses to them, and wave a fond farewell. But they don't take the motorbike down right away. She's already turned away, walking toward the front entrance, and their heads bob as they follow the rhythm of her footsteps, caught in the wafting scent of breakfast at Tiffany's that my sister seems to emanate, before heading back downstairs to resume inhaling carbon monoxide.

By now, Sara has looked up and seen us: she waves at us with both arms. Clearly, my mother wasn't waiting for Sara, she was waiting for that wave: she shoots over to the apartment door to buzz the downstairs door open for her.

At the same time, I turn off the light and press closer to the glass, so that I can see all the way down to the end of the street: the brewery, the smokestack, and the terrace with the six huge letters held up by iron cross-shaped pipes, like on a building in Manhattan: P E R O N I. I light a cigarette while I listen as my mother carries Luca in triumph to the door, and the door opens.

Sara comes over to say hello to me, the little boy gobbling her neck, and then she steps into the bedroom to change. I can hear Luca letting her do everything she needs to, and a wave of fury sweeps over me, because if I had tried to do the same things, he would have squirmed like an eel in the kitchen sink on New Year's Eve. I crush out my cigarette and go to join my mother in the kitchen. She has one burner occupied by the pasta and chickpeas, one by the pan with the cutlets, and one by the coffee pot. Anyway, we can't eat until Alfredo gets there. It's only eight at night.

"I've been thinking, while they're working on your apartment, you could come stay here."

"Mamma, it's not like I don't have a place to live. While they're working on the apartment, I can live in it."

"You want to camp out in the middle of that mess? When you have a home right here?"

"You already have Luca here all day . . ."

"But that boy is crazy *about you* . . ."

"That may be true, but he also *drives* me crazy."

Mamma gives up trying to understand, she lifts the lid of the Moka Express coffeepot, and adds sugar.

"Ask Sara if she wants any."

Sara is rubbing Luca's feet on her face, her back is turned to me.

"You want coffee?"

She shakes her head, touching her stomach. My sister is an admirable woman: if she has an acid stomach, she does without coffee. I'd sooner do without my stomach.

Luca is so crazy about me that he insists on sitting on my lap while we eat dinner. He fishes in my bowl for dark chickpeas with one hand, because my mother told him that they are lucky. That authorizes him to plop his hand in my food, it authorizes his father, his mother, and his grandmother to laugh as they watch him, and it obliges me to suffer in silence.

"Today, I was going through my jewelry box, and I found Aunt Vanda's earrings."

I already know where she's heading with this, at regular intervals, those earrings pop up everywhere.

"You really ought to get your ears pierced . . ."

"Mamma, I'm thirty-eight years old, do you really think I'm going to get my ears pierced now?"

"Your Aunt Vanda is going to go to her grave without the happiness of seeing those earring in your ears."

"I swear . . . I have to get holes punched in my ears, otherwise my aunt is going to die heartbroken . . ."

Sara wipes her plate clean with a slice of bread: "Mamma, do you think this is the right time? With all the things she has to get done?"

"Why, she's not doing the construction herself, is she? Isn't Alfredo's contracting company doing the work?"

I listen to them, as they talk about me in the third person.

"The company doesn't *belong* to Alfredo: Alfredo works there. It's Gianni's company, but anyway, you wouldn't understand: you got married in this house, and you've never left."

They give me a ride, because every so often they actually go home. Alfredo walks ahead to get the car out, while Sara and I, strolling arm in arm, follow about twenty steps behind him. We walk along the sidewalk: sitting on motorbikes, the new generation of the "third world" do their best to conquer their midweek isolation. A small cluster of them blocks the corner of the sidewalk where we need to step off into the street, and so, physiologically, Sara and I part ways: I step into the street and walk around them and the parked cars, while she continues straight ahead, and as she does, gathers her hair into a ponytail with the elastic she has wrapped around her wrist. The cluster of kids draws back, splitting in two to let her pass, without a word.

When we are about to turn onto the Vallone di Miano, there is a sudden and overwhelming odor of fermenting yeast.

My father's clothing had that smell the day he walked toward me in the brewery courtyard, the day that a rat had run through a classroom at our school, and we had all been sent home early, and Mamma had said: "Let's go pick up Daddy at work," and she had waited outside the courtyard and I had zigzagged through the brewery workers letting out on their lunch break, and at the front door of the plant I had seen my father removing a white hair net from a woman's head and kissing her hair.

I'd never seen my parents kissing each other that way. It wasn't cheating, because he wasn't repeating the same gestures with another woman: that father was a different father, a different man, a different thing. All the same, I turned to look at my mother, and I felt certain that from her vantage point, she had seen it too. And so, in order to keep from taking sides, I stopped exactly midway between them. Until my father left the doorway and walked toward me.

That night, on *Canzonissima,* we watched Carlo Dapporto telling jokes I couldn't understand.

I was in a state of expectation: something was about to happen, something was about to change that evening—change forever.

But nothing happened at all.

My father laughed, but he couldn't explain the jokes to me. And when my mother started laughing too, I started getting scared.

Then Mina appeared.

From a panel on the top right, Alberto Lupo, with a neckerchief, was telling her all the right words, in the old song *Parole Parole*. But she had already heard all those words, and she could perfectly well do without them. She could do without chirping crickets, the full moon, bouquets of roses, and it was only by doing without all those things, even without him, that she was able to sleep and to dream.

Dad died years later, falling off a ladder while polishing a copper still. The Peroni brewery observed a minute of silence before sounding the siren. On the day of his funeral, they held a union meeting, so that his closest friends could get away long enough to come hug us. Aunt Vanda told Sara about it, certain that she was too young to fully understand death. But Sara understood, and she screamed loudly.

That scream was enough for us to raise his body and close it up in the coffin, to withstand the priest's drawling sermon, walk behind the coffin all the way to Poggioreale, bury it in the ground, on the spot where eight years later we would stubbornly go ourselves to rub his whitened bones with alcohol, return home, and resume our lives. Archive our father in any old niche of our memory. That scream was enough to ensure that there was nothing more to say. It was the broken pact, the failed promise, the path abandoned halfway through. It was a parent with offspring not yet fully grown who indulges in the irresponsible lightness of death.

"If you drop me off here, I'll go get cigarettes at the vending machine."

"Okay, good night."

"'Night."

And so, one day the black-market came to an end. Those who were already born when the Allies landed could never remember a time when it wasn't part of our lives. But then one day, without warning, it was gone. Without leaving beggars in its wake—no one died of hunger, no one was left without a trade. There were no shoot-outs, no shops shuttered and dark, there were just minor renovations like the one that Enzo was doing. And then vending machines began to appear, but there had been a lengthy interregnum during which we had lost all our benchmarks, all our points of reference.

9 A.M. to 6 P.M., with lunch break

The workmen buzz me awake on the intercom. My kidneys hurt and my back is killing me. I step out onto the landing in my underwear, I call the elevator, and when it reaches my floor I open the door and leave it ajar. I wash my face over the mason's bucket, then I use the same water to flush. The stench of the city rises from the toilet.

I close the elevator door and release the car, thinking to myself that my stomach will be able to handle the anti-inflammatory after I've had my coffee, and the vodka fumes that waft in along with the workmen only confirm the soundness of that decision.

I roll up my sleeping bag so that I don't come home to find it dusted white like a Christmas manger, and I admonish the contractor : "I'm closing this door, and the sleeping bag's staying in this room; you'll tell the workers, right?"

"Well," he responds, "I don't know, today we have to replaster the ceiling in that room too."

"No, Gianni, if you get that room all damp too, then where am I supposed to sleep?"

"I could bring you a pup tent."

I smile at him, but then I fume inwardly all the way from the front door to the subway entrance.

"Weekly pass," I say.

And I plunge forward into the muzaked Tchaikovsky provided by the Naples Transit Authority. There's a woman who has taken refuge in the furthest nook at the end of the platform, right under the speakers: I walk down the ramp slowly, to keep from spoiling her enjoyment of *Romeo and Juliet*. It's the end of Act II by the time I realize that that corner of the platform is the only place where you can smoke a cigarette without being caught on the security cameras. Without a voice breaking into the adagio to tell us that smoking is prohibited. I squeeze myself onto the ledge next to the lady and light a cigarette of my own.

After twenty minutes of watching the blinking signal in the signboard marked "Destination: *Pozzuoli—Solfatara*," the woman decides that her love of Russian Romanticism will not withstand the ordeal, and she heads back to the surface to catch a taxi. It doesn't matter to me, I'm chased out of my own home anyway early each morning, and it doesn't end here: after this, I have to take the C21.

The video display on the C21 beams out advertising for whoever thinks that's a good place to put their advertising, along with a daily horoscope. My horoscope is lousy, but as I'm stepping off the bus, it's showing the horoscope for Taurus. Taurus isn't bad: I appropriate that astrological sign for the day, and I go to the shop.

In the morning, before the shop opens, this is how we are: we keep our distance from one another at first. While all the other shops are still closed and the bank employees take espressos in disposable cups wrapped in aluminum foil up to their office, we amuse ourselves with cell phones and cigarettes. We cling to our private thoughts, the thoughts that we will leave shut tight in our lockers, jammed in between our watches and badges, thoughts we won't have again for many hours.

We know that what awaits us is a kind of work that won't be enough on its own to constitute another genuine form of thought. And so we stand there, before the shop opens, dawdling a little longer. Like a woman who spends her life in the company of a husband she no longer loves, and if there's a minute to spare, she takes that extra bit of time at the door of the lover she won't see again for the rest of the day.

After that, we let the day wash away around us: we're there, in the shop, and our work gives us nothing, and we can't give anything to it except for our time, with a constant awareness, like a background noise, that we are betraying ourselves.

We smoke in the bathrooms. Maria and I split a cigarette; I sit on the john, she's leaning against the door, as if we were back in school. Then we wash our hands and brush our teeth.

As the lunch break draws near, our weariness turns into euphoria. It begins to waft through the departments, it hurries down the stairs. In the locker rooms, it takes the form of lipstick, ponytails loosened around the shoulders, strawberry-colored thongs bought at a sale, yoga breathing exercises, boiled vegetables in an aluminum container for Rosaria's diet, photographs of the kids we left with their grandmother taped to the doors of the lockers, deodorant under our armpits, and premenstrual sobbing.

I walk past the administrative office while the chief accountant tells Sergio that he made a mistake issuing an employee badge. I hear Sergio answer him: "Okay, well then fire me: I don't have the courage to quit."

The accountant laughs, but I know that Sergio isn't kidding: I invite him to come have lunch with me.

"Okay, but only if we buy *panini* and get half an hour of sun . . ."

It's going to be one of the last half-hours of sun, I can't bring myself to deny him this pleasure: September is tumbling down onto our heads, and without there having been any months we can look back on with longing.

Perched on the rocks overlooking the beach are us shopclerks; insurance adjusters, with their ties loosened, taking off socks and shoes; and junior attorneys wearing wraparound sunglasses and holding the latest-generation

Blackberries. Below us, the beach umbrellas are furled, but girls who look like sumo wrestlers are stubbornly singing the latest neomelodic pop songs as if it were July, as if they were Mina on a chic Tuscan beach.

"Whenever I skip my August holidays, September is just a month like any other."

"September is never a month like any other."

"Why, what happens in September?"

"In September, I want to live in Paris."

"When have you ever been in Paris in September?"

"Never."

"When have you ever been in Paris?"

"Never."

"Do you speak French?"

"No."

"So?"

"So, nothing, it's just that . . ."

So, nothing, it's just that if I were in Paris in September, I wouldn't sweat. I'd walk briskly through the grey air wearing a carded wool overcoat, and I'd pay no attention to the yellow linden leaves underfoot: I'd know instinctively they'd still be there the next day.

I beckon to the Singhalese guy: I've decided I want a three-Euro tattoo. Sergio and I leaf through dozens of possible patterns in the loose-leaf binder: tribal motifs, and felines in every imaginable pose, roses big and small.

"I can write a name, if you want . . ."

"How about a phrase?"

"Like 'I love you'?"

"Like '*Will those Tartars ever get here?*'"

"That's so long . . ."

"True, it is, but we're not going to write 'What the fuck,'" and I hand him five euros.

Sergio flattens the paper that the sandwich was wrapped in, and he writes on it: the Singhalese tattoo artist copies with a fountain pen filled with henna.

While he writes on my shoulder, I bore Sergio to death with my complaints about the renovations, the workmen, the contractor who keeps trying to be a comedian: "I never should have moved, even if it was over with Lucio."

"But that's not why you moved . . ."

"I swear, it's been years since I've had a halfway decent boyfriend."

"So get a completely indecent one."

"They're all indecent. No-o-o, I'm sick and tired, I tell you, Sergio, I've gotten old, I'm weary: I'm dreaming of an arranged marriage."

"But you can choose . . ."

"No, I'm dreaming of an arranged marriage in a society where all the marriages are arranged, so that I don't even have the shadow of a doubt that it's less than perfect. You get it?"

"You shouldn't joke about something like that: think of how many women's lives were ruined by that sort of marriage."

"Okay, but at least when they think about it, they know it's not their fault."

"Anyway, if you ask your mother to find you a husband, you know she'd get right to work . . ."

No. But that wouldn't be enough. I'd have to go back to virgin territory. I want never to have seen him falling asleep in our bed without knowing why. Accepting that days could go by without wanting to make love. Discovering that our love has become that light vise that squeezes without pain, that still lets you move as before, just slower, more laboriously.

I could never want that for myself. I want shouting matches, slamming doors. Departing footsteps on the stairs, never to return. I want last acts, with spectacular finales, the truth screamed into your face. Sex, for the last time, so it hurts. I want to despair, because our love wasn't over. There was still enough left that we could scratch some off the bottom of the barrel. I want to be left brutally, a thousand times, abandoned, my place taken by another woman.

Instead, one morning I looked at him, sleeping in the bed, and I knew that I no longer loved him. And I couldn't believe it was true, because that love had been my existence for years, my only choice, the only way of making it to the end of the day.

To understand that a love has consumed itself and come to an end is tantamount to an admission that you are no longer the person you once were. You are stunned, like a child abandoned by its parents; you sleep as if you were in an orphanage. It's a test of one's existence that engenders many new life forms: suitcases packed, never to return, consciously settling into boredom, lovers, friendships into which you pour your slumbering energies, job changes, career incentives, lots of children. But no one who has understood what happened will ever forget that life has branded them with one of most unhappy signs. A sign that lives on in the often furrowed brow, the yearning when you look at young people kissing in the park, as you hinder your own children from plunging into love.

*

"It's starting to itch."

"What is?"

"The tattoo."

"So scratch it. Should we grab a quick coffee?"

"No, let's head back, we'll drink an espresso at five: otherwise, we've thrown away even that last straw of hope . . ."

But before five o'clock rolls around, my professor and thesis adviser comes into the shop, and finally I know that I can tell her. I watch as she walks into the store, moving past the shelves, lightly touching items on the counters; she disappears behind a pillar, reappears, and then walks briskly toward me. Finally I can tell her that I know. That just a little over a year after my degree, one day, while leafing through a book at the office of education, I had noticed a footnote, a footnote that referred to another book; and the book was by her, by Marta Vassalli, the woman who served as my thesis adviser. I ordered the book and it arrived, express delivery, two days later, and then I sat down and read the entire second half of my thesis, the section with the experiment and conclusions, the section that earned me my summa cum laude, the part I had sweated out, night after night, on the keyboard of my Olivetti Lettera 22, the words that my mother swept up the next morning, crumpled up on the floor among the cigarette butts: and there it was, my thesis. Finally, published, a real book, with footnotes and bibliography, printed in 12-point type, notch-bound, cover price twenty-eight euros. Author: Marta Vassalli.

And now, there she is, right before my eyes, and I can tell her, straight to her face, easy as pie: *you're a thief*, but somehow I can't do it, I smile a full-time smile at her, and wait for her to speak.

"Ciaaaao, is it really yo-o-o-o-ou?"

"Yeah, it's me, more or less."

"And now you work he-e-ere?"

I amplify my smile, using every muscle known to mass-market distribution, and I wave before her the leash I wear around my neck, the one that holds up my badge, marked with my name, but only my Christian name, just a hint at the surname, cut short after the first letter by a period: full surnames are used for the authors of books, shopclerks don't need them. I smile at her, and I grip the badge: if I happen to get lost, in the store, at least I'll know my own name.

"But this is a lovely, lovely, lovely place to work."

"I'm not sure I'd go that far . . ."

"Listen: not everyone who gets a degree can do research . . . or teach . . ."

And that's true, not everyone who gets a degree can teach. And many of those who do teach shouldn't be allowed to do so. I wanted to teach in junior high school, and only there, because the age of twelve is a terrible thing—not something you can get over without help. That rapidly deforming body, that wave of pubertal sweat, needs someone, and there must be someone after all, who can explain why you shouldn't take up smoking, that your father didn't die because he fell in love with another woman, that your mother wasn't happy to see him die, and that she didn't kill him by remaining silent.

"Sure, of course, the main thing is to have a job . . . Was there something special you were looking for?"

And as I look for that something special that she is incapable of finding for herself, I know that I've heard the things she said so many times that I almost believe them.

Something of the sort must have passed through my mother's mind the day I was hired, the day I came home and threw myself down on my bed. My mother called my Aunt Vanda in her excitement; even with ears buried under my pillow, I could hear her relief: "A full-time job, *with benefits*."

She left the house that afternoon even though it was raining, and her shoes still weren't dry from buying groceries. She went straight to the jeweler's shop and purchased an ex-voto.

I didn't know that my mother had ever prayed that I be given a grace, and of all the ones she could have asked on my behalf, certainly not that one. I never found out what church she left it in, or what it depicted: I never asked because I was so deeply offended.

But even now, whenever I go back home, I walk into churches and peer into chapels, prying with my eyes among the shrines and cases and statues. Painted wooden saints hold out their arms like coat racks, festooned with all the hope and prayer that they have managed to gather, and I wonder where my mother's ex voto might be, I wonder what form she might have selected for me.

A pen, a hand, a head, a book with three letters puncturing the silver: p.G.R., "per Grazia Ricevuta": my condemnation and my resignation, "for Grace Received."

I light a candle and I toss a euro for myself into one of the boxes, at random.

Half an hour before my shift ends, Gianni, the contractor, calls me; he doesn't beat around the bush: "The joists under the bathroom floor collapsed."

"Well, it sounds like they didn't just collapse: you made them collapse."

"Well, anyway, there's no floor now: shall we take this opportunity to move the sewage line?"

"What the fuck are you saying? What the fuck do I know? How bad is it? . . ."

"Huh? Who?"

"The bathroom, how bad is the collapse? Now who's going to pay for this? Don't move, I'll catch a cab and come take a look."

Evening

From the taxi, I send a text message to Sara, I explain what's happened, and tell her to send Alfredo over to my apartment immediately. Alfredo is already there, she writes back, and then maybe she thinks it over and adds that she's on her way, she'll be there immediately.

"Nothing serious."

"What if someone had fallen in?"

"No one fell."

"Sure, but do you have these workers on the books? What if someone had fallen in? What if there had been someone downstairs?"

"Alfredo is on the books."

"How come you only answer half of the questions I ask you?"

"Because you ask too many questions all at once."

"Alfredo, blessed Christ on a Cross, you talk to this guy . . ."

Sara shows up to calm me down, she kisses her husband, she looks down through the hole in the floor, into the bathtub of the woman downstairs, and whistles in astonishment.

"Did you see that? She has a whirlpool . . ."

"And I don't even have a toilet."

"Ah, don't worry about that, they'll rebuild your bathroom in a day, but now go and talk it over with Gianni, this is an opportunity to put the fixtures where we want them: you can have the toilet wherever you like."

"How about on a floor. Does that sound like a good idea to you?"

"Come on . . . they promised they won't go home tonight until they're done fixing it . . ."

I make my way through the bottles of solvent and the bottles of vodka; a workman gestures for a cigarette, I hand him the whole pack, tell him to keep it, and then ask him for one for myself.

As I look down onto the lavender-colored bathrobes of the woman downstairs, we choose a location for the toilet, for the bidet, and for the sink. Gianni pulls the tape measure from my finger to the corner: "But if I put your bathroom sink here, I can't install a light over the mirror."

"That's better, it means I won't have to gather my courage to look at myself every morning."

"You mean the wrinkles?"

"But I don't have wrinkles, I don't have wrinkles. Do I have wrinkles?"

"No, of course you don't. And it's nice to look at you, in the morning."

" . . .Where's Alfredo? Alfredo-o-o? Who's going to pay for all this?"

I appoint Alfredo to catch the woman with the whirlpool, downstairs, when she comes home and faints, and I flee with Sara.

We drive up the main thoroughfare, heading for the hypermarket to do Mamma's weekly grocery shopping.

"Gianni really likes you, he likes your hair."

"What does he know about hair?"

"He likes curly hair."

"I like straight hair."

"When Mina wore her hair curly, you liked your hair . . ."

"When Mina wore her hair curly, I *was* Mina, my hair was *her* hair."

I turn to look out the window, the great industrial sheds of the packing plants, North African women gathering around bonfires, unfinished overpasses, apartment buildings overlooking the highway, and we are on the road looking up at the apartment buildings, and the paved lots with cars lined up in rows, their windows fogged over even if it is only September, and I can't even remember the last time I made love.

"Whenever I used to make love . . ." I begin, "from time to time images would unreel before my eyes, in no particular order, just like the things you see from a train window."

"Ah, so you do like him . . ."

"Like who?"

"Gianni."

"Oh, cut it out."

"Anyway, me too."

"You too what?"

"I see snapshots, too; scenes appear before my eyes."

"But you've been married for ten years . . ."

"True, but I've been seeing beaches and waves for twenty years . . ."

When she was fourteen, Sara came home from boarding school for Christmas break, and I went with Aunt Vanda to meet her at the station. Aunt Vanda waited in the car, triple parked, and sent me in to help Sara with her luggage: when I got to the track her train had come in on, there was Sara, kissing Alfredo. With that face covered with zits so you couldn't even see the color of his skin, I thought, isn't it disgusting to kiss him? No, it didn't disgust her: she wanted him. She wanted him and no one else, she'd spend hours locked in my room with me, forcing me to listen as she talked about him. Our mother picked up on scattered clues and began to inquire suspiciously. We picked up on her signals, and instinctively gave misleading answers.

But Sara was collapsing under the weight of her secret love: outside was our mamma, an object of fear because no one had ever come back home with such a raging fever of lovesickness, but inside and everywhere was Alfredo, growing, feeding off every minute that passed while they were still apart, struggling against the concealment, the secrecy, until finally Sara exploded and spilled everything. Mamma learned that Alfredo was just sixteen, but had already been working full-time for four years. He was a bricklayer.

After an abbreviated, non-jury trial, our mother and Aunt Vanda decided that Sara would not be allowed to leave the house for the rest of her vacation, that she and Aunt Vanda would accompany the lost soul back to boarding school on the train: Rome's Termini railroad station, taxi cab, Via Nomentana, at 6 P.M. on January 6th.

Sara said nothing but: "I want him, and he's mine," and as she said those words, her right hand closed like a fistful of talons, and she flew straight up into the air, clutching her prey.

Sara stopped studying, then she stopped eating, but she didn't die. Two years later, in his first automobile, Alfredo drove the two hundred and fourteen miles from Naples to Rome and drove her out to make love.

As they lay in an embrace on the reclinable car seat, Sara saw the beach, the waves.

She saw the beach at Gaeta the way it looks through the window when the train spits you out of the tunnel and you know you're almost home.

Luca was born out of this, and now he moves through life with the confidence that you see in those who learned how to swim when they were babies, before they could even feel fear. People who float comfortably along on the surface, bobbing offshore for hours, doing nothing at all, turning occasionally in the water, admiring their feet, and when you swim out to where they are, floundering and out of breath, you realize that they aren't even tired, in fact you can lean on them and rest for a moment before swimming back to shore along the shortest possible course, as perpendicular to the beach as you can manage.

"No, what I see is cities, scenes of cities that I've visited, foreign cities . . ."

"Reasonably attractive."

"Sure, they're attractive, but I just don't understand what connection there is . . ."

"No, I mean Gianni: he's reasonably attractive."

"I can't say whether he's reasonably attractive, but he's demolished my apartment."

"That apartment had problems."

"I know . . . I know, but I shouldn't have moved, even if it was over with Lucio."

"But that's not why you moved away . . ."

I didn't move. I was evicted.

I was walking out of the subway at ten minutes past noon, I had just turned my cell phone back on, crossed the street between a Smart car and a Fiat Punto, and I was walking up Pignasecca, under the scaffolding for the restoration.

"Hello."

I knew it was Lucio because I had seen his phone number on the display an instant before I answered, and an instant later a hand had reached down to grab it, trying to jerk it out of my hand and run off with it.

But my grip was too strong, my hand had developed muscles, strengthened from the work at the store, the twelve hours of inventory on January 7 of every year. I had pulled back, tugging downward on the arm and the cell phone, I'd reinforced my hand with my other hand, and then I'd continued: I'd snapped back my elbow with all the strength of surprise and I'd punched him in the stomach, right in the sternum, exactly where the bones of the ribcage leave the vital center unguarded. The boy had folded over like a towel being put away in a linen closet and fell to the ground.

That's when I did it. That's when I started kicking him in the face, in the head, and screaming: "YOU CAN'T DO

THAT, YOU CAN'T DO THAT," and then I went on screaming, just screaming. But not just any ordinary scream: that moaning voice that I hear when I'm crying, that vibrating breath that's what I fall back on when I know that it's better not to ride the words if you want to go on living.

They gathered us both up off the sidewalk, me, completely exhausted, and him, bleeding, fourteen years old, and unconscious.

They took me to another hospital, in a state of shock; when they finally discharged me, facing charges of excessive force in self-defense, with Lucio as my defense lawyer and ten eyewitnesses who swore backwards and forwards that I had done exactly the right thing, I went to visit the boy in the hospital.

At the entrance to the ward, his father had managed to restrain himself: it might have become a city where a woman can beat a young boy half to death, but it was still a city where men don't punch women.

His wife spat on my shoes.

"Get out of here, get out of my sight."

I left; I got out of her sight. I had been acquitted because I had never been in trouble with the law, I had a full-time job, a bank account, a college degree behind a sheet of plexiglas at my mother's house. And also because the newspapers had been talking about a *crackdown* for months, and the national government sent the army down to stand guard in Forcella and the Spanish quarter so that Americans who wanted to spend some time ashore during their Costa cruise could go shopping without fear.

But the neighborhood sensed the truth. Everyone knew that there had to be a reason that I had made it out of the "third world" addicted to no drug worse than tobacco, while that boy was in and out of reform school; that at the age of fourteen, at ten past noon, he was not sitting impatiently at a school desk waiting for the bell to ring, but instead was waiting for me to loosen my grasp on my last gift from Lucio; that, one way or another, I had made it to age thirty, and beyond, while it was uncertain whether the boy stretched out unconscious on a sidewalk would ever make it past tomorrow.

What that reason might be, and where it lay hidden, no one could tell me, but that reason made me stronger than him, and it meant that I was guilty of abusing my superior strength.

The neighborhood thought the same thing I thought. And, little by little, it isolated me in a vacuum of silences and things left unsaid, people began to forget to invite me places, to involve me in things, even to say hello when I greeted them, and it finally spat me out, the way a lame dog will amputate its paw, its leg, biting away at the limb it no longer recognizes as its own.

I moved out and I paid Lucio's legal fees, because I knew I'd never see him again.

The scent of hops wafts over the balcony only in summer, or on evenings like this one. When it was too hot to study during the daytime, that scent told me that between me and those workmen tightening and loosening valves a generation was passing. Now I know that we have gone backwards.

"Luca!" I call through the glass. "Luca!" But he knows that the reason I'm calling him is to point out that my purse isn't reversible, and that I was not very happy about finding it turned inside-out like a pillowcase.

I knocked on the glass-paned door and called his name. "I wanted to play *regbi*."

"You wanted to play rugby?"

He had me now. I should have started right in with You-know-that-you-shouldn't-touch-things-that-don't-belong-to-you. But he's turned aside my righteous anger: he's launched into a description of the rules of the game, muddling rugby with baseball, and my purse with a catcher's mitt. First-class leather. Then he loses interest and wanders off, unscolded.

"This child is spoiled rotten," I say to Mamma.

"Leave him alone," she says. "He's such a good boy."

And in fact, now he's good as gold, he talks to himself, completely immersed in a game that no one else understands. He's doing the same thing I do when I'm alone in this apartment, or when I'm in the other apartment, in the elevator, in the bathroom: I talk, when no one else is listening, discussing things that only I know about. I become the me that could have given a better answer, the me who knows how to ask questions, the me who dies and has someone to mourn my death, who has someone who left without asking, and is now coming back to ask forgiveness. Now I'm Mina, gazing down as Alberto Lupo kisses her hand. The woman who wards off applause and congratulations after teaching a masterful lesson, who walks back and forth on the bathroom tiles, rehearsing a better entrance, a brighter smile, a more sensuous gaze.

And I do it to make up for the past.

Alfredo comes back from my apartment. He's exhausted, his T-shirt is smeared with plaster. He hurries in to take a shower, as he walks past he smoothes my furrowed brow, a gesture to tell me not to worry. Sara doesn't even need to glance at him; she transmits gratitude and contentment in his direction.

"There's something written on your shoulder."

"It's a tattoo."

"Jesus, oh Jesus, now she's got a tattoo."

"It's a fake tattoo, Mamma, it'll be gone in two weeks."

"Now, you tell me: a tattoo you can get, but Aunt Vanda's earrings, no?"

"Mamma-a-a?!?! It's a fa-a-ake, it washes off with water . . ."

"So? Are the earrings permanent? If you don't like them, you take them out and the holes seal up by themselves . . ."

"Mamma, let her be: she has other holes to worry about sealing up right now."

"Madonna, it's true, Alfredo, what a disaster . . ."

"Oh come on, it's not a disaster, it'll be fixed by tomorrow. You want a ride?"

"No, no, I'll take a bus."

"I don't understand. Why does she have to leave right now?"

"No, you know what work's like . . . I have a nine-hour shift tomorrow . . ."

"Eh, and can't you sleep here? You don't even have a toilet where you live now . . ."

"Mamma, I may not have a toilet. But I have to leave. Now. Right this second. Now."

"But at least eat something before you go."

"I'm not hungry."

I travel through the "third world" with a compelling

need to escape from the outskirts of the city. The outlying areas are designed to force people to stay shut inside their houses, but what I need now is a downtown, and people who feel like they are suffocating indoors and go sit outside on the streets.

Gripping the handles of the R5 bus, I can see one thing clearly: I will never become Mina in the song "Parole Parole Parole." Maybe I could become Mina with children, Mina grown fat, Mina learning Chinese so that she can sing a song without getting the pronunciation wrong. But I'll never be Mina who coyly eludes Alberto Lupo's compliments, who easily outreaches him by three full octaves, and then surrenders to him in the throes of passion.

I'll never enjoy the black and white certainty of the close of broadcasting at the end of the day, I'll never step off the stage to go end the soirée in a restaurant frequented by the after-theater crowd. I'll always remain the little girl who went to bed in a floor-length gown and pouffed-up hair, who refused to wash her face to keep from ruining the mascara, so carefully applied by the make-up artist, the little girl who fell asleep with high-heel shoes on her feet. The last thought before drifting off into slumber: a bouquet of red roses, sent by Alberto to the most elegant dressing room in RAI-TV's Studio 10.

"Excuse me, would you like to sit down?"

Christ, I must be old. I'm Mina, but old now, unrecognizable, riding wearily along the Corso Garibaldi in a bus with ten junkies making their way home. "Sure, thanks."

I look down, and it's Gianni.

"Have you eaten?"

"No."

"Want a pizza?"

*

I hold the fried pizza so tight that the oil drips down my hands, Gianni wipes my right wrist before the drop of oil can reach my sleeve.

"Oh, it needs washing anyway," I say.

Then, I reject my annoyance and reluctance, and I swallow all the distance along with the bite of pizza, and I turn to look at him. I hold the hand that cleaned my wrist, and right now I don't know what else to do, but this hand built my house. I know this hand. I bring it to my lips, I kiss it lightly, a kiss that consoles me but means nothing. No messages, no winks, no flirtation, no fucking. I kiss it gently, meaning nothing but thank you, or help me, which has always been the same word to me. Now I can no longer look at him, but I have this hand raised to my mouth, I stroke my right cheek with it: it is rough and swollen. It is the first caress I can remember, my temple, my forehead. I can feel my face only on the back of his hand. When I pass it over my eyes, I have said everything: message, winking, flirtation, fucking, but also thank you and help me. I kiss it once again and then I let it go. He looks at me. He says nothing, he does nothing, He looks at me.

The apartment is freezing. It's even damper than in the street. I feel like lighting a cigarette, but my pockets are crammed with objects of all sorts, my badge, my membership in the film forum, my discount card for highlighting at the beauty parlor. Gianni walks through the apartment in the dark, and plugs in the cable we're using to tap power from the streetlight outside the window. I stumble over the tools piled near the front door, the neat piles of cardboard boxes filled with clothing, the designer tiles from Aunt

Vanda, and I am forced once again to accept this man's hand for support. He squeezes me tight where my hips taper inward toward my waist, as he kisses me he tips me backward, but there is nothing to be done, because he is in control of the center of gravity of this embrace. He knows the slope of the floor, the give of the joists, the rust on the fixtures. I say nothing, I only tremble.

Later, the snapshots begin to stream past.

The first thing I see is a cupola. It looks like Lisbon at first, but then, little by little, I realize that it's Santa Egiziaca at Pizzofalcone.

The corner of Via Case Puntellate, just after the earthquake.

The post office behind the flea market at Antignano.

Mergellina, one evening in the damp interior of a boat, dressed in a long skirt.

The Ponti Rossi aqueducts, on the way down from Miano.

Piazza Borsa, when there was still a fountain.

The prostitutes at Carbonara.

A large front door, seen from above: maybe it's the Stella quarter seen from Corso Amedeo.

The Pisacane dock, near the trolley stop.

The entrance to the Trianon, seen from the terrace of the pizzeria across the way.

The top of the staircase outside the Central Post Office, when kids hurl themselves down the steps in fruit crates, and I think that it must take too much courage or recklessness to allow yourself to hurtle down all the way to the end, and I always close my eyes and deep inside, I say: "No."

"Yes, why not say yes? Why *no*? Yes." Gianni is speaking softly into my ear, holding me tight by one wrist, and sliding all the way down with me, next to me as I fall. Afterwards, we pull the sleeping bag over us and fall asleep, without even having a place to pee.

ACKNOWLEDGMENTS

The first page of this book was written immediately after a telephone conversation with Matteo Codignola, which went more or less like this:

Matteo: "What are you doing?"

Valeria: "I'm writing a short story for an agenda."

Matteo: "And why are you wasting time writing stories for an agenda?"

As I write this, I still can't say whether I should thank him.

Without doubts, I thank:

Sandra Infante, because she lends me her eyes for reading; Nicola Lagioia, because he picks at details, without being a nitpicker; and Francesco Russo, Francesco, Francesco, Francesco: for everything that concerns us.

About the Author

Valeria Parrella was born in 1974 and lives in Naples. Since the publication in 2003 of her debut short story collection, *Fly and Whale*, she has been widely regarded as one of Italy's most exciting young authors. Parrella is also the author of the novels *The White Space* (2008) and *The Verdict* (2007).